Calvin Miller

Frost

A Novel

BETHANYHOUSE
PUBLISHERS
MINNEAPOLIS, MINNESOTA

Frost
Copyright © 2002
Calvin Miller

Cover design by Dan Thornberg

Published by Bethany House Publishers
A Ministry of Bethany Fellowship International
11400 Hampshire Avenue South
Bloomington, Minnesota 55438
www.bethanyhouse.com

Printed in the United States of America

Library of Congress Cataloging-in-Publication Data

Miller, Calvin.
    Frost / by Calvin Miller.
       p. cm.
    ISBN 0-7642-2364-X (alk. paper)
 1. King of Prussia (Pa.)—Fiction.   I. Title.
    PS3563.I376   F76   2002
      813'.54—dc21

                                                    2002010131

As with snow, wind, and shade,

so with frost,

to Melanie

CALVIN MILLER is a poet, a pastor, a theologian, a painter, and one of Christianity's best-loved writers with over thirty published books. His writing spans a wide spectrum of genres, from the bestselling SINGER TRIOLOGY to *The Unchained Soul* to the heartwarming novellas *Snow*, *Wind*, and *Shade*. Miller presently serves as a professor of preaching and pastoral ministries at Beeson Divinity School in Alabama, where he and his wife, Barbara, make their home.

There is often a single glimmer of sanity before a failing mind shuts down. So it was with Mabel Cartwright. "Would you just look at that! Mary Withers's house is up for sale." This was the first lucid thing Mabel had uttered in an entire week. It was also the last lucid thing she would ever say. She resembled a comatose soldier waking briefly from a battlefield nap. Awake for but a moment before going back to sleep forever.

Christine was encouraged by her mother's brief visit into the world of the sane. She hoped that perhaps this meaningful statement was a sign that her mother was getting better.

"That's good, Mama!" After having lived with her mother these past four months, she had come to feel that a working mind was a thing to be complimented. "Yes, the house is for sale. The rumors must be true; she's not coming back to King of Prussia." She spoke loudly and distinctly, trying to goad her mute mother into a conversation. But Mabel was not only through talking, she was somewhere off the planet. Only her body remained on Earth. But Christine was suddenly desperate to see her well, so she decided to try a more elementary course. "What's my name, Mama?" she asked.

"Ummm . . . Olivia?"

"No, Mama, I'm Christine. Olivia was your sister who died in 1919, remember?"

"Nineteen . . . nineteen?" said Mabel. She said the four syllables as though it were a Congolese word she must unravel using some remote linguistic key. Mabel seemed to be turning the date over and over in her head, as if by repeating it she might grasp its meaning and then be given the fog light to move with greater speed through other mists in her mind.

Mabel was alone, though she had no idea what the word *alone* even meant. And because Mabel was alone, Christine was also. She knew all too well what the word meant. In fact, she had begun preparing herself to be alone for the rest of her life.

Mabel and Christine were walking home from the market. Mabel was just walking. They were together as Christine saw it. But Mabel was past any notion of togetherness. She was neither together nor alone, for such words and their distinctions could only be conferred on those who possessed the ability to define, to explain.

Christine's life was not rich with relationships. She had supported herself in the streets of the Big Apple until the hard times had come, when she returned to King of Prussia penniless. She was what the good Lutherans of King of Prussia called a "fallen woman." Of course, if her mother somehow had the mind to think clearly of her daughter again, she would never have thought of her that way. Still, some things can wriggle through the smallest openings of the brain and emerge as insight.

Mabel blurted out another question. It was for Olivia or Christine or for anyone in earshot. An odd question from an absentee mind: "Are you pregnant, Olivia?" she asked.

"It's me, Mama. Christine. No, I'm not pregnant."

The early fall evening bisected the road with the lanky shadows of two women whose thin frames appeared as bent wire hangers for the faded dresses they wore. Their trip to market had been taken in quest of a pound of lard. Christine had only the most meager of resources. The lard she carried, along with the dab of flour they had left, would go together to form a piecrust. The summer sun was moving away from the town, the days shortening into cooler nights that awaited the coming frost. The welcome rains of September had ended the recent drought. It was a traditional Pennsylvania fall, and the drought-shrunken apples were plentiful. Sugar, like lard, was now harder to get and near impossible to afford. But they had a little of both. Cinnamon too. So they would make an apple pie. Maybe two, and afterward search for an answer on how to come upon their next meal.

Christine felt both ashamed and grateful that her mother's mind couldn't grasp the question she had asked. She was ashamed she had lied. For she was pregnant. What kind of woman would lie to her poor demented mother? She knew who the father was, and when her pregnancy became obvious, all who lived in King of Prussia would suspect who it was. It had happened. She paused. "It" was how she referred to the conception of the child she carried. There would be no doubting it. Her August fling with the Bible salesman would soon make her dingy reputation even more stained in the community. Her manner of dress had told them all that she'd once been a "lady of the evening" during her New York years. The pregnancy would only add to the disdain with which she was already regarded by most everyone. But her mother's failing mind in some ways made her perpetual embarrassment easier to handle.

Christine studied the side of the road as though contemplating the gravel would give her mind a relief from the heavier things it couldn't bear. Frankly, she was scared. The baby would come in May. The winter was sure to be a bitter one. The hope of any help from the welfare organization during the depression seemed even colder than the weather. She was a woman of frozen hopes. She had been unable to locate the Bible salesman and knew that even if she could find him, it wasn't likely he would admit to being the baby's father. Any kind of child support was out of the question. The only people in King of Prussia who had the means to offer her a job were the McCaslin family, but the backfire of her recent blackmail attempt with Peter McCaslin eliminated that possibility.

As they approached home, Christine realized there was almost nothing in the pantry. The baby would not only be undernourished while in the uterus, it would be born into a world of hunger. Christine glanced down at her starving body, at her bust in particular, and wondered if there would be adequate milk to feed her newborn child. Although it was too soon to worry about that yet. For now there was lard.

The old Victorian house to which the two women were headed was already drafty and cold on this autumn morning. For a moment she wondered if she could go back to the streets. Then she looked down at her soon-to-be-enlarging abdomen and shook her head. The streets of Manhattan? No. Poverty was more easily endured in a small town. The city streets had once yielded the income of one-night stands, but they had always left her colder in the mornings. She faced the truth. The streets were full of younger women whom she couldn't compete with anymore. And the hard times had made bargain shopping common, the competition fierce.

She must be honest with herself—her youth was about gone. Her shape was about to change dramatically. Besides, she had an unborn child who needed her because she didn't know her own name, with a mother who fit the same description.

Yet somehow Christine felt a kind of thrill in seeing herself in a new way. She had nothing, it was true. But she was needed now. She felt needed in a way she'd never experienced before. To be needed was a wall against the hunger, against the impending winter. She smiled.

Which felt good; she hadn't done it in days.

So it was on that October morning, Christine had been given two giant reasons to remain in the world: a demented mother and an unborn child. At first she had thought about aborting her baby, but then she had grimaced at the idea of hurting the little life she'd spawned. It was her own recklessness that had conceived the child. So it would be her own more penitent responsibility that would enable her to care for it. Suddenly she was ashamed of her earlier thoughts of getting rid of her unwanted child. It wasn't an unwanted child. She wanted it and God wanted it. God wanted all children. She smiled again. After all, she wasn't the first mother to question her body's ability to make milk in a land devoid of milk and honey. Life worldwide was hard. Children died of starvation every day. Just how much did God want them in His starving world? Who could say? Yet want them God did.

Not only did she have a reason to be in the world, she was here to help God take care of two souls who couldn't take care of themselves. It was up to an ordinary person like her to assist God in keeping these helpless ones alive, moving forward. Yes, in this matter even an ordinary prostitute could do some good. Life can be wonderful, something to be cherished, even when it is unwelcome in the world. Even when it is hungry and cold. It is the well fed and warm who seem to feel that the hungry and cold are better off dead. Not so. To Christine, it was better to live hungry and cold than never to have lived at all.

She suspected her pregnancy was now at the center of a local gossip blitz. The nurse at the local doctor's office wasn't known for keeping confidential information to herself. Christine would likely be shunned by the "good folk," those who would number her among the bad. She figured, however, that having a spotless reputation would do neither her mother nor her baby much good. A new way of seeing herself came upon her all at once. Christine Cartwright, on this crisp October day, transcended her need to be listed on the social register of her hometown. There was work to do. Though the work would be lonely, it was still most important. Friends and reputation are both nice, but when a person knows why she's in the world neither of them are really necessary.

Exhilarated, she reached the front porch of her mother's house. No, not her mother's house but her house. Strange how she'd once thought it looked like an old haunted mansion. Now it throbbed with life. The shingles hung about the roof at odd angles. Here and there they were too split to hold out rain. There was a leak in the corner of the master bedroom, which she would never be able to afford to fix. But for all its disrepair the house was beautiful. Like Christine, it appeared old and deprived. Even so, the place had purpose, as did she. They would both live out their purposes together.

As she swung open the front door, greeting her was a most wondrous sight. There on the dining room table was a twenty-five-pound sack of flour, a can of baking powder, two ten-pound sacks of sugar, a cake of yeast, and a huge tin of lard. There were also two bottles of milk, thin and blue at the bottom, rich with golden cream at the top. It was a day of miracles. There was no meat, but in 1930 meat was hardly ever available and seldom of very good quality when it was. Nevertheless, with flour and sugar and yeast, meat wasn't all that necessary. Apples were of more importance to Christine, and she'd already stashed baskets of them down in the fruit cellar.

She surveyed the groceries. There was no note, no God bless you. *This can't be from any church*, thought Christine. *Churches always leave Bibles and some sort of flyer on "how to be saved."* Yet she knew that every anonymous gift leaves the one receiving it feeling somehow indebted to the giver, most especially to God.

But Christine and her unborn baby and Mabel too hadn't eaten much in the past week, and the best way to thank God was by expending one's hunger on a good meal. For sure Christine had that. "Mama," she said, "I'm not much in the kitchen but I think I'll cook us up some potatoes and make a pan of biscuits!" Christine cast her eyes down then at her flat stomach and said, "Well, Baxter, I've got to eat for the both of us. Sure hope you like biscuits."

Mabel could not have interpreted her daughter's words even if she had heard them.

Why Christine named her baby Baxter the town would quickly guess, remembering it as the last name of the baby's father. How she knew her unborn child was a boy was a mystery to her. She knew it because she knew it. Because she could not think of her child any other way. She knew it because Benny could not have sired the other gender. She carried a boy.

Christine could not help but wonder how many other children the Bible salesman had sired. Still, thinking of Benny Baxter gave her no pleasure. Thinking of biscuits did. She reached for a mixing bowl and then picked up the baking powder and hugged it to her chest.

Looking toward the ceiling, she exulted, "Here's to us—you and me, God! There are three people depending on our friendship, and two of them don't know it."

Otto found his daily trip to the mailbox the most disheartening of activities. Twice he had received letters from publishers saying, "Dear Mr. Mueller, while your work is exceptional, it does not meet our publication needs at this time." Or, "We regret to inform you that we cannot publish your work because . . ." Still, Otto reasoned that publishing poetry was the stuff of dreams, and the present economic times now a hard reality.

Even as he walked to the mailbox, he wondered if Ingrid and Erick had perhaps overrated his writing ability. He didn't feel all that talented. Until just recently he hadn't shown his poetry to anyone else beyond the small circle of his immediate family. It seemed unwise to let anyone else in on his dreams. If too many knew, it might keep his work from being published. Besides, he wasn't sure their enthusiasm was any real confirmation of his ability. *People sing,* he told himself, *whether or not the theatre is empty. They sing because that's what singers do.*

He opened the mailbox and pulled out three letters. None of them was from a publisher, but there was a check for $147 from the power company. It was good they used Mueller coal to make electricity, and so very nice that they paid. Another was a letter from Ingrid's sister in Oneida. They hadn't seen her since Hans's funeral, though she had written them faithfully every week since to assure them of her emotional support. The final piece of mail was from their coal supplier, requesting they send some more of the money they still owed on the huge stockpile of coal they had left over from the previous spring, which had turned out to be much warmer than anyone expected.

Now that Otto was more in charge of things, he felt the same burden Hans had always felt and even found himself secretly praying for a cold winter. Otto tried not to dwell on the happiness he would feel if he ever did get a positive letter from a publisher. He imagined himself opening the mailbox and erupting with joy as he read the letter of acceptance of his manuscript. But this would not be the day.

"Any significant mail, Otto?" asked Ingrid

when he reentered the house.

"A check, a bill, a condolence," he replied.

"The stuff of life—checks, bills, and condolences," Ingrid said as she stepped into the living room. "I wish one of them was a letter for you from a publisher."

"Mama, is it possible your exuberance over my poetry has deluded us both? Maybe I'm not as good as you think I am."

"Well, Erick thinks so too, and he's a professor at the university."

"But he teaches mathematics, not literature."

"Otto, you're a poet! Now don't argue with me. The letter and contract are probably on their way already. When the mail comes tomorrow, you'll see for sure I was right all along."

"I'm afraid no poet has ever risen from eastern Pennsylvania."

"So that's it. Can anything good come out of Nazareth? That's what Reverend Stoltzfus said in his sermon just last Sunday. Jesus was a great man with a forbiddingly small address. So are you, Otto. You'll see."

"Mama, I'm going over to see Isabel," said Otto on his way out the door.

Otto knew Ingrid didn't like the way he abruptly finished his conversations. She wanted him to stay and argue with her till she won the argument fair and square. It wasn't so much that Otto doubted her. He knew that what she said was true—he never finished their talks. He preferred leaving them and tried to remember where, to take up the subject again whenever he pleased. Only now he didn't please. He pleased to see Isabel, so he vaulted into the coal truck and headed out toward the dairy.

When he arrived there, he was delighted by the smell of coffee that wafted through the half-open door. He raised his hand to knock on the door, and before his knuckles could meet the wood, Isabel was at the door. She grabbed his rap-ready fist, pried open his hand, and placed a warm scone in it.

"Come in, Otto. Have you had breakfast yet? If you say yes, I get the scone back!"

"The answer is no." Otto held out the scone. "How about putting a little cream and jelly on this, if you don't mind."

Isabel didn't mind. Soon Otto and Isabel were sitting at the table facing each other, mug to mug. "Had the mail come before you left?" she asked.

"Yes," said Otto in a dejected tone that let Isabel know there was no answer from a publisher. "Isabel, I don't think they like my book."

"Not true! They just haven't read it yet. To

read it is to love it. Have you written anything new lately?"

"No, not yet. I'm in a slump. Whatever I write sounds like claptrap."

"Not possible."

Wanting to get off the subject of his writing, Otto asked her, "I was thinking, do you think your brother likes me?"

"My brother likes my brother. Peter adores Peter. It's a small circle of devotion, and he's fervent about it. But why this sudden interest in whether or not Peter likes you?"

"To be honest, there's been a lot of talk at church about our getting married someday and I just want to be sure both our families feel good about our relationship. When we get married—"

"By the way, Otto, when exactly are we getting married? I'd like to know. I want to try to schedule it in if I can," laughed Isabel.

"Isabel, I haven't yet saved the money for a ring," he said, clearing his throat nervously in an attempt to shift the conversation away from date setting.

"I know, but we don't need a ring to get engaged. Lots of people make promises and keep them without ever exchanging expensive jewelry." She stood to get more coffee.

Otto put a spoonful of the clotted cream on

the raspberry jam and watched as the red and ivory colors swirled over the edge of the scone and ran down onto the saucer. "These are wonderful!" said Otto to Isabel as she returned to the table.

"If you want, I'll make them for you every morning once we're married," she said.

"I do, I do," Otto laughed, then took a healthy bite of the delicious scone. After chewing a bit, he said, "It looks like your old boyfriend will be a father in a few months."

"I heard that rumor too. And it's the very kind of father that Benny would be, without the burden of being a husband and provider." Isabel looked past Otto and out the front window of the house. It was a mean comment and sounded a little odd coming from Isabel, who by and large never criticized. But it seemed a fair thing to say, and Isabel didn't take it back.

"Do you think he's slept with every woman he's befriended?" Otto suddenly realized how incriminating his words must have sounded to Isabel. He quickly added, "Except you, of course."

"Otto, I hope you don't think—"

"No, no, I don't think that. I just wonder how a man who sells so many Bibles can ignore so much of what it teaches. You would think he'd find some decent models somewhere in the Book."

"Solomon had 750 wives and 250 concubines."

"Well, he didn't pick 'em up selling Bibles."

"No, he didn't," agreed Isabel. Weary with talking about Benny, she asked, "Otto, how is Marguerite's cold?"

"Better. She'll be her regular self in no time."

"You think Marguerite is ready to have another mother? Or that I'm ready to be one?"

Before Otto could reply, Ernest Pitovsky came crashing through the door, not bothering to knock. He was clearly in an agitated state.

"Miss Isabel! Miss Isabel!"

"What is it, Ernest?"

"You've got to come right away! It's Helena . . ."

"Yes, I will, but tell us what's the matter!"

Ernest made no answer. Instead, with a confused look on his face, he turned and hurried out again. Without hesitation, Isabel jumped up from her chair and followed. Otto limped as fast as he could to keep up with the both of them, but they far outdistanced him as they ran toward the dairyman's shack.

When Otto finally arrived, he saw Ernest and Isabel hovering over a very sick woman. There were splotches of blood on the linens, a pool of it on the floor. Helena was coughing, her coughs coming out strangled and broken as she gasped after life. There was a terror in the moment that clearly registered on the faces of the two Pitovsky children, Katrinka and Freiderich, who both stared wide-eyed from a dark corner of the small house.

Isabel wasted no time in taking charge of the situation. "Otto, help Ernest get her to my house! I'm going to call Dr. Drummond." In a matter of minutes Otto and Ernest stood in the entryway of Isabel's house with Helena in their arms. She was barely breathing.

"Come in, come in!" shouted Isabel, holding her hand over the phone's receiver. She was obviously waiting for Dr. Drummond to come on the line. "Put her on the couch," she said and they did. Seconds later Isabel was talking to Drummond.

Otto and Ernest tried to piece together their telephone conversation just from listening to Isabel. "You can't do her any good? . . . No, don't take her back to the sanatorium . . . You can meet us within the hour at the county hospital . . . You think that this is best? . . . All right then, we're on our way."

Isabel hung up and glanced at Otto, who had a hopeless expression on his face. Poor Ernest, a big man, was kneeling beside his wife, fighting to keep the best part of all he was alive and in the world. Helena never looked more frail, more weak.

Just then, Katrinka and Freiderich appeared in the doorway, both sullen and frightened. They had been kept alive by a caring father and mother, the hospitality of friends.

Otto thought, *Surely, Lord, if one family has had more than their share of heartache, it must be this one. Please, do something to help them.* Then he realized God was doing something. There was Isabel. Isabel, whose gift of love to the Pitovsky family remained the one link between hope and desperation.

"Let's go! We'll take the dairy truck," said Isabel.

Ernest, the children, and Otto all crowded into the back of the truck. Isabel got behind the wheel with Helena gently placed opposite her in the front seat. She was slumped against the worn upholstery of the seat, her husband's hands on her shoulders to comfort her and keep her steady.

Otto watched everything taking place before him with a feeling of awe. Sure, he could play with words and phrases. He could arrange them, move them around, make them sing, dance, and weep. But then there was Isabel. He loved a woman who worked with the angels.

She could manage hardship, stand up to evil, and somehow bring forth some good. What Otto did with mere words, Isabel did with lives. Yet she didn't give of herself without it taking a personal toll. It seemed to Otto that she paid dearly to help save her world. With each attempt to help others live, she herself appeared to die a little.

Sitting quietly in the back of the dairy truck, Otto held the frightened children on his lap. Otto tried to still their shivering by caressing them but found this didn't work. Katrinka and Freiderich kept right on trembling even as he embraced them. He thought of his own Marguerite, recalling how scared she'd been when her mother died, how the child had sobbed, unable to understand the deep sorrow that enveloped her.

Before too long they were pulling up at the hospital. A strong Bavarian-looking woman dressed in white worked with Ernest to move Helena from the front of the truck to a waiting gurney. Ernest kissed Helena's limp, pale hand and then followed the nurse who wheeled his wife into the hospital and down the antiseptic corridor.

After parking the truck, Isabel and Otto and the children made their way to the emergency waiting area where they found Ernest sitting in a chair in the corner of the room. He was weeping. When Katrinka and Freiderich saw him, they too started to cry. They rushed to their huge father and grabbed on to his shaking form.

Isabel crossed the floor and touched Ernest on the shoulder. She said nothing.

Helena's condition was serious, even critical. But Otto knew that whatever happened, God had an ally on this earth who would act on His behalf and do all she could to help heal. Otto was in love and knew right then they would marry soon. He must not postpone their union any more days than was necessary. As he studied Isabel helping Ernest, he realized it would take the rest of his life to learn all that Isabel was, and that he would gladly do it.

Sometime midafternoon the nurse approached Ernest to tell him what he already knew, that Helena wasn't doing well. Although she seemed to be out of danger for the moment. They could go home for a while, she said.

Ernest wouldn't hear of it. "Miss Isabel," he said, "about the afternoon milking . . ."

"Don't you worry about that, Ernest. You stay here with Helena; the dairy will be just fine. I'll come and get you later tonight. Meanwhile, we'll take the children back to the farm and get one of the women at church to look after them while Otto and I handle the chores."

During the drive back to the farm, Otto found a coal delivery form folded and stuck away in his pocket. He took out the form, unfolded it, and turned it over. It was clean on the back. And any clean surface became an opportunity for Otto, the poet, to sing.

Life hadn't been easy. His mind raced back in time to old memories. He thought of his war injuries, of his late father's rejection of his enlistment. He thumped his stiff leg, rebuking it for not handling the war any better than it did. He remembered Renee's death and Marguerite's terrible situation at the orphanage. Thoughts of Hans's death just two months earlier came flooding in and smashed like the waters of a broken dam against the memory of his needy homecoming at Christmas.

But mostly he thought of Isabel. Over the past months he'd watched her single-handedly hold the Pitovsky family together. This poem would be for her.

He pulled out a stub of a pencil from his shirt pocket and let the dull graphite point glide across the back of the coal delivery form. The lead did its work, and Otto scratched out his celebration of love to the one driving the dairy truck as it rumbled down the highway with Freiderich and Katrinka fast asleep in the back.

Is it true you are a milkmaid?
Only this and nothing more?
Then the milk is human kindness.
Where is that Bethlehem that birthed you?
That Nazareth that watched you grow?
How came you to this little place
So weepingly in need of grace,
Healing even as you go?
I love you, for you never count the cost
Of giving others life by dying some yourself.
Come, marry me and let me help you make
A pageant of disdain
By using deaf-mute actors
In a theater of pain.

Isabel, the couch is not a butcher's apron! It looks like you slaughtered a sow on the Chippendale!"

"I'll clean it up," offered Isabel. She spoke softly and in a conciliatory way that she hoped would calm her furious brother.

"You can't clean it up. Blood is the hardest thing in the world to get out of damask."

"I'll have it reupholstered, then."

"You think it's that easy? That you can just replace the couch Grandmother McCaslin brought here from Scotland a hundred years ago? I don't understand you. What gets inside that head of yours?"

"Peter, Helena had a relapse. She was hemorrhaging badly. I'm afraid we may lose her. I just don't know how much more that family can stand."

"I just don't know how much more I can stand of that family!"

"I don't want to have this conversation again. You can't just throw a family like this to the wolves. Besides, Ernest is doing a good job. He's one of our best employees. I left his children with Mrs. Stoltzfus until he gets back from the hospital later tonight. They have beautiful children, so bright, and yet they always seem afraid."

"I'm sure they're geniuses, but the world is too big for you to take care of everyone on your own. You've neither the stamina nor the money. With all the money you spent on Helena Pitovsky when she was at the sanatorium, Ernest must be the highest paid employee we've ever had. Think of the expenses they've required! How did these drifters ever become our responsibility in the first place? And now his wife has bled all over our furniture. Isabel, you're a fool! When will you ever learn?"

Isabel could see that her conversation with her brother was going nowhere. Most every argument she had with Peter couldn't be won. It wasn't even possible to get him to look at things she considered to be important. Peter's perspective was just that—Peter's.

"Did I get any mail today?" she asked.

"A couple of letters. I put them on your bureau."

"Thank you." Glad the conversation was over, Isabel hurried to her room and shut the door behind her. She picked up the letters, immediately recognizing the penmanship of the one on top. Benny Baxter. She had the sudden impulse to toss it in the trash unread. She was resolved that there was no admiring Benny, and the only way to keep herself from being frustrated by his memory was purposefully not to think of him. She had managed to do this pretty well, at least until she overheard someone speak of him. Or, as in this instance, when he wrote her.

She decided to read the letter. The decision to read it seemed an act of nobility. She tore the end off the envelope and pulled the folded pages out and was amazed to see two twenty-dollar bills tumble to the floor when she unfolded the pages. Reaching down and picking up the money, Isabel stuffed the bills into her pocket, flexed the two pages of the letter in her hands, and began to read.

Dear Izzy,

You've probably heard by now that I've left the Scranton area. I felt the Lord leading me to Cincinnati. There have been hardly any committed Bible salesmen through here so there is a lot of spiritual darkness. You may not know this, but Cincinnati is a dark city desperately in need of

Bibles. So I feel I've been sent here to help bring the light of God's Word to this city.

I've heard about poor Christine's misfortune. She is with child, and I am sure the whole town is abuzz about her condition. "Behold, she is with child by whoredom (Genesis 38:24)." I was hoping that after she read from the Three Generation Regal Heritage Bible, *she would give up her loose lifestyle. But God's Word did not take root in her and now the seeds of her sinfulness are soon to bear the devil's fruit. For a time I dated Christine trying to turn her from her carnal ways, but alas my godly example had little effect on her entrenched lifestyle.*

Dear, dear Izzy, in seeking God's will, I believe He wants me to help Christine with her little one, and so I am sending you the first of three small offerings to help bring the child into the world. I know Christine's money is tight, and what I am sending will not go far, but it should be enough if she has her baby at the county hospital. You can still have a baby there for around fifty dollars. I want to ask you to save the money here enclosed. I will send you some more each month to put with it. Then when it is time for the child to be born, she will be able to pay the hospital bill and perhaps buy the child a much-needed layette.

I know Christine would be reluctant to receive money directly from me, as she is trying to make me believe that I am the father of the child. But I believe she would receive it from you, especially if you can find a way to give it to her anonymously. As long as she doesn't know where the money has come from, she will gladly receive the help.

With this letter I raise an Ebenezer of trust (it's in 1 Samuel 7:12), for thus far the Lord has been my help. I know you will not fail me in this matter. I am convinced that God wants you to help me help Christine. If only poor foolish Christine was as chaste as you and I. Harlots are an abomination and will have their place in the lake that burns with fire, although maybe Christine will become a Christian and then live more as I have always taught her. Thank you. I know I can count on you.

> *Sincerely, Benny*
> *Jesus is my King!*
> *Bibles are my thing!*

Isabel had mixed emotions about Benny's letter. She knew he was lying. She had seen him and Christine leave a bar together one night, both of them drunk, and had come to her senses about this odd Bible salesman who doubtless was the father of Christine's unborn child. Isabel expected that he had a Christine in every town he visited. She knew that the forty dollars was little more than blood money, a clear indication of his guilt.

Nonetheless, she also knew that Christine

would need help, and there would be none to help her when the time came for her baby to be born. The dairy farm was all but broke, most of their customers hopelessly behind on their payments. And the extra padding of their once ample bank account was now depleted. They managed to pay the help most of what they owed them each week, but very little was left at the end of the month for the McCaslins to live on.

Strange, thought Isabel. *Just two bills and yet it's been so long since I've seen this much money.* Most of their customers paid in ones or in silver coins. Without thinking, she folded the bills and stuck them in her pocket, where the money remained the rest of the day.

After milking and completing her work in the separating room, she realized she must stop, grab a sandwich, and then head back to the hospital to pick up Ernest Pitovsky.

Within the hour she was back at the hospital, where she found Ernest still sitting in the waiting room. His face lit up when she walked through the door. He stood and gave her a rib-crushing hug with his huge arms.

"Things must be better," said Isabel. "Your face hasn't had that kind of smile on it in a long time."

"Yes, the doctor told me Helena is resting

much better now. He thinks she'll be able to go home in a week. But they want payment in advance and I don't have any money, so I don't know what to do. She's got to stay till she gets better."

"How much are they asking for the week?"

"It's horrible, but they want forty dollars! Now, where am I gonna get forty dollars?"

"Forty dollars?"

"I told the doctor it might as well be forty thousand."

"Forty dollars?"

"Miss Isabel, why do you keep repeating it?"

Isabel reached in her pocket and took out Benny's money for Christine. "Here, Ernest," she said. "This money just came to me in the mail. This must be the reason why."

Soon Ernest was sitting in the front of the dairy truck, with Isabel behind the wheel, and they were driving home. They rode in silence a great deal of the way. Finally, Ernest asked, "Miss Isabel, do you think our whole lives are predestined by God, or are we just stumbling into the things that happen to us by chance?"

Isabel was in no mood to talk of such a heavy subject. Still, it was one of the most serious things she'd ever heard Ernest say, and a question that needed to be answered. "Well, the Lord knows the end from the beginning. So, however hard things get for us, they are never baffling to our heavenly Father. And the miracles of God which overwhelm us are just ordinary work in heaven."

"Does that mean if I need exactly forty dollars and you have exactly forty dollars, that it was a miracle and that God wasn't surprised by it?"

"Maybe."

"But you said that—"

"It depends on where I got the forty dollars."

"Did it come in the mail just today?"

"Just today. But it wasn't exactly given to me to use as I choose."

"You mean it was money sent to you for another reason?"

"Yes, but I'm sure God doesn't mind that I used it to help you. I'm just borrowing it for a while. I'll get it back some way...."

"I promise to help you get it back. I sure hope God doesn't mind you using it to help Helena."

"Ernest, I'm not here to speak for God, but I know how much He loves Helena and I know how much you love Helena."

"And Freiderich and Katrinka, they love Helena too. In fact, with her so sick, I've had to ask myself what would happen to them if she didn't pull through. All in all, I'm glad for the forty dollars. Probably God doesn't mind, and for sure I'm grateful."

"Probably He doesn't mind."

The rest of the trip passed in silence.

Back at the dairy later that night, Isabel looked up at the ceiling of her dark room. "God, I sure hope you don't mind that I used Benny's money for another reason. I promise you, I'll pay you back. God, I've got to try to help the Pitovskys. I need to reupholster the Chippendale too. I need to do a lot of things and they all cost money. God, I can't afford to wait around to get most of this done. Everybody needs help and there are a lot of things to look after. I sure do need you. You're not mad, are you, God? It was a little dishonest, but I'll pay it back. Until I do, will you help Helena to get better? Then there's Christine. Help her not to have her baby early, and above all, not until I get Benny's forty dollars replaced."

Before Otto had gotten back to the coal yard, Ingrid was surprised to see Erick arriving home from the university. He had walked from the train station to the office, which Ingrid tended every afternoon. As he walked through the door, Ingrid looked up and saw that he was very pale.

"Erick! What are you doing home in the middle of the week? Is everything all right at the university? What's the matter?" She jumped from her chair and went to him and embraced him. "Why, Erick, you're burning up. We've got to get you home."

He was shivering, and his teeth were chattering. She thought of the killer flu back in 1918 and was suddenly afraid. Since Hans's death, she had a fear of all sickness, as it was generally the first step in the act of dying. Further, Ingrid had heard that polio was the new dread word that had become attached to flu and colds.

"Can you walk good? Are your legs working?" The two questions were one and the same. The answer was obvious, the question unnecessary. Erick had just walked from the station to the coal yard. His legs were fine. Yet this was how polio manifested itself, with adults as well as children. It had even struck such a notable Democrat as Franklin Delano Roosevelt.

"Mama, it's just the flu!" It was the first complete sentence that Ingrid had given Erick time enough to say. "I'll be all right, although I don't feel very good right now."

"The flu can lead to other things. Just look at poor Franklin Delano Roosevelt." Ingrid had always loved the governor of New York's middle name. "Just proves," she went on, "that even important people can get bad sick."

"Mama, I'm going home. Where's Otto?"

"He's been over to the McCaslins' all day—clear through lunch. Doesn't look like he'll be here when Marguerite gets home from school."

"He's got it bad, doesn't he?"

"I'm afraid he's got something more terminal than the flu. But she's a nice pretty girl with a soul of all things fine and good. I think even Hans wanted them to marry, and before he—" Ingrid's voice was stopped by the rush of emotion. It was still too recent, and she was still too fractured inside to be healed. She stood silent while her eyes "glistened up," as she liked to say, then she blotted them at the corners and said, "Let's get you home, son." She grabbed her purse and keys and, with her free hand, nudged Erick through the door. She locked the door and then they walked together to Ingrid's house. Once there, it wasn't long before Erick was in his bed resting.

Later, when Marguerite came in from school, Ingrid insisted that she stay away from Uncle Erick.

"Why, Grandma?" asked Marguerite.

"Because he's got the flu, and flu can lead to worse things."

"Like polio?" Marguerite was knowledgeable for a first-grader.

"Well, yes, like polio."

"Our teacher said they'll probably need to close the swimming pool next spring so we don't get what Mr. Franklin Delano Roosevelt got."

"I should say so," said Ingrid. She felt proud. How many first-graders could say *Delano*?

"Erick's snoring, Grandma."

"That's good. Erick needs to sleep. Sleeping will help him to get well."

Marguerite nodded in agreement.

"Marguerite, let's go to the store and buy ourselves a chicken. When Uncle Erick wakes up, he'll be needing some hot chicken soup. And here's a penny for you to buy a Tootsie Roll."

Marguerite was delighted. Ingrid twisted the lid off the old cold-cream jar where she kept her grocery money, and then she and Marguerite were off on their short outing.

The house was filled with the aroma of a fat boiling chicken. "I've got a theory, Marguerite," said Ingrid. "The fat is where the health is. So when you get older, if you find yourself cooking a chicken for a sick friend, be sure you get a big fat chicken, okay?"

"Okay, Grandma. Please can I eat the Tootsie Roll now?"

"I told you, after supper. It'll spoil your dinner."

"Grandma, I have a theory about Tootsie Rolls. I think they're better'n chicken fat to help you not catch the flu."

"Your theory is not yet proved, child. Give me the Tootsie Roll. I'll put it where it won't tempt you till after dinner."

"Do I have to?"

"Yes, you have to," said Otto, who had

slipped in from the back porch.

"Daddy! Daddy! Uncle Erick's home and we're cooking a fat chicken to make him well, and I get a Tootsie Roll after dinner. Franklin Delano Roosevelt caught polio, but Erick's only got the flu. So we're all going to eat chicken fat because—"

"Whoa! Slow down, Marguerite. Mama, is Uncle Erick really home?"

Ingrid nodded, and Otto walked straight for Erick's bedroom. Ingrid heard his steps slow as he approached his brother's bed. Ingrid could hear them talking.

"Hi there, brother."

"Otto . . . hi," Erick said groggily.

"Feeling bad?"

"I've felt better."

"I'm afraid you're in for chicken soup tonight. We're all in for chicken soup tonight. It's not fair. The rest of us feel fine."

Ingrid imagined Erick smiling at his brother's attempt at humor.

"Sssssst!" hissed Otto. "I nearly burned my hand on your forehead! You're hotter than a January poker."

"How's your love life?" asked Erick.

"Sssssst!" he repeated.

"Hotter than a January poker, huh?"

Ingrid tried not to listen, but she heard all

their words. She knew Otto was being extreme and that Erick still carried a deep love for Mary Withers to the point he'd been suffering from depression over it. He lived daily with the hope that she would return to her house and they would pick up where they left off in their relationship.

"Go back to sleep now, you need the rest," said Otto. "We can talk about my love life later."

"Ssssst!" Erick said as he closed his eyes.

Ingrid enjoyed the pleasant sound of the chicken bubbling in the pot and the homey odor it created. She busied herself in the kitchen, occasionally clanging a pot or clinking a dish. Otto settled in with the newspaper while Marguerite looked at the pictures in a children's book she was too young to read. Except for Erick's sickness, it seemed a pleasant evening. Ingrid felt uneasy but fulfilled. She went back over the day in her mind and remembered she hadn't seen Otto for most of the day.

"Otto, why were you ... I mean, where were you today?"

Otto pushed the newspaper to one side. "I went out to see Isabel and then to the county hospital."

"Hospital! What for?"

"While I was visiting with Isabel, Helena

Pitovsky took a turn for the worse and started bleeding pretty bad. She was deep in trouble, so Isabel called Dr. Drummond and—"

The doorbell rang.

Ingrid waved Otto into silence and went to the door.

She opened it, and a look of shock swept across her face. For a second she was too stunned to speak. She smiled, then warmly laughed. "Mary Withers! Alexis! Do come in."

"May I come in too?" asked the man standing just behind them.

The smile left Ingrid's face. "Well, yes, Ted. Please, do come in." It was clear that Ingrid had welcomed Mary in with a great deal more enthusiasm than she had Ted. To cover this, she smiled brightly and all but overdid her charm, repeating to him, "Yes, of course, Ted. Do come in!"

"Hello, Otto. Hi, Marguerite," said Mary and extended her hand.

Rather than shake her hand, Otto, with a bow and flourish, kissed it.

"A poet to the last!" Mary said, and they all laughed.

"Marguerite!" cried Alexis.

"Alexis!" shouted Marguerite. The two six-year-olds ran to each other and met with the kind of impact that nearly toppled them both.

With some awkwardness Mary and Ted took the chair and couch that Otto and Marguerite had vacated. After greeting them, Otto sat down in the maple chair in the corner.

"Coffee?" asked Ingrid.

"No, thank you," said Mary. "We mustn't stay long."

"Surely you have time enough for a cup of coffee?"

"No, Ingrid, please," Mary insisted.

Ingrid quickly dropped the subject of coffee and said, "Mary, it's nice to see you in King of Prussia."

"How's Erick?" asked Mary, then acted as if she wished she could take back the question. "Ted and I have come to close the house—"

"Erick is not doing so well," interrupted Ingrid. "Since you left, he hasn't been the same. I think your leaving and his father's passing have been too much for him."

"Ingrid, I'm sorry. What I regret most is not staying after the funeral. I've felt so guilty that after all you and Hans and Erick did for me and Alexis last winter . . . I should have at least spent some time with you after the funeral."

"Mary wanted to be here, Mrs. Mueller. I'll vouch for that," said Ted. "But . . . Mary and I are in love, and people do funny things when they're in love!"

"We sure do, Teddy dear," Mary said, though with a tone that didn't match Ted's in its enthusiasm.

Teddy dear, thought Ingrid, *how very corny*. What was it about Ted that had drawn Mary to him? She wasn't sure. To Ingrid, he smiled too broadly, and though handsome, there was something in his appearance that disturbed her. Why had he waited so long after the funeral of Mary's husband, his own twin brother, to contact her? Years had gone by. Had Mary heard much from him during that time? Ingrid could only recall one instance when Mary had mentioned "Teddy dear," saying that he was out of touch with the family and that they had no idea where he was.

It was a brash kind of return that he had suddenly made to their world, King of Prussia. So Ingrid ignored Ted Withers's little explanation about how people do funny things when in love. To Ingrid, Ted came across as serious and conniving, not some giddy adolescent who was lovesick. She knew she could be wrong about people, but she felt certain she was right this time.

Ingrid returned to what was for her a much better subject. "Erick is in the next room," she said. "He's desperately sick at the moment."

Mary nervously studied Ted, who had

instantly become restless when he learned that Erick Mueller was in the same house. He cleared his throat and said, "Mary, I think we'd best be going. We have a long drive ahead of us." Ted stood then and nodded toward the door.

"You're right, of course, Teddy dear," Mary replied, standing.

"Don't you even want to know what Erick's sickness is?" Ingrid asked. "Have you forgotten how much Erick cared for little Alexis when she was so sick last winter?"

"I'm sorry. Forgive me, Ingrid. You're right, no one could have been better to me and Alexis when our world seemed to be coming to an end. Erick was more than wonderful." At Mary's words Ted's eyes appeared to flash his disapproval. Mary went on. "He is indeed a wonderful man—always concerned about others. Of course I want to know the cause of Erick's sickness."

"Mary, we really should be going," said Ted before Ingrid could answer. "Alexis, come, we have to go!"

"Yes, come along, Alexis," said Mary. "Time to go now."

Ingrid was surprised to see Mary suddenly turn on her heel to leave, responding instantly to Ted's rude behavior.

Alexis put down the book she and Marguerite had been happily looking at and protested, "No, I don't want to, I want to stay here. Can't we see Erick? Can't we stay with Uncle Otto and Marguerite?"

Ted gave no answer but instead walked across the floor to where the girls were playing and abruptly jerked Alexis upward. The child grimaced in pain yet didn't cry out. It was when Ted grabbed and lifted her that Alexis's pinafore flew up far enough for Ingrid to catch sight of the dark blue bruises on her upper thigh. Then the child looked pleadingly at Ingrid, clearly wanting to be out of Ted's iron grip.

"Mary, whatever caused those bruises on Alexis's leg?" said Ingrid.

"Let's go!" Ted insisted.

Mary obeyed him, but as she turned to leave, suddenly her eyes filled with tears. "Good-bye, Ingrid. Good-bye, Otto, Marguerite," she said.

Before Ingrid and Otto could say good-bye, Ted and Mary were at the door. With Ted carrying Alexis roughly through the door, the child continued to look backward with begging eyes.

"No, no!" said Erick, bursting from the bedroom. "Mary, please don't go! Mary, life here is not possible without you!"

"Erick!" cried Ingrid. "Please, you mustn't be so forward."

Sick as he was, Erick stumbled forward, as if to rescue Mary Withers and her child.

Otto ran to him to stop him. Grabbing him by the shoulders, he said, "Erick, you're not well, please!"

Erick shook loose from Otto and charged past Ingrid and threw open the door. Ted, Alexis, and Mary were just outside and walking away. "You can't treat a child that way!" Erick shouted to Ted. "Get your hands off Alexis!"

"You're out of line, pal," said Ted. "This is *not* your child, and Mary will *never* be your wife!" For a moment both Ted and Erick looked like they were ready to start throwing punches at each other. Ingrid and Otto stood there watching, both of them wide-eyed at what was taking place in front of the house.

Then, turning to Mary, Otto said, "Mary, Erick is sick. He has a fever and wouldn't be behaving this way otherwise."

"He's sick all right!" shouted Ted. "He's real sick! They've got places for people with his kind of sick! You'd better keep him under control, because sick or not, if he touches my family—"

"He didn't mean any harm, Ted," said Mary cutting him off. "And we're not a family yet."

Ted's response to Mary's comment was to grasp her arm and begin leading her away. Ingrid saw then the reason for Mary's pain. She was afraid. What had Ted threatened her with that had led to such a terrible situation for Mary, that he would lay claim to her life like this?

"Mary, I'm so sorry ... so very sorry," said Erick, then he started to sob.

Erick's outburst had brought about a tortured response in Mary. The tears in her eyes increased now and began spilling down her cheeks.

While holding Alexis, Ted Withers led Mary to an old truck, which appeared to be loaded with Mary's personal belongings from her old house.

Otto gently closed the door, and the three of them watched through the front window as Ted just about shoved Mary and Alexis into the truck on the passenger side and slammed the door behind them. He marched around the front of the truck, swung himself into the cab, and once again slammed the door. Starting and revving the engine, he put it into gear and roared out of the driveway, down the street, and was gone.

"Mother, Otto, forgive me. I was out of my head," Erick said, turning to them. "I'm so ashamed; I know I embarrassed you both. And poor Mary, I pray she will forgive me. But I can't help loving her. I can't quit loving her. She must not marry that man. He's a horrible human being. I don't care if he looks exactly like Tom, he can't be anything like him. I know Mary well enough to know that whatever made her love her late husband is missing in his ogre of a brother."

Otto and Ingrid nodded. "Erick, you have to let Mary go," said Otto. "You must be prepared to give her up, even to a man you think is despicable. Life doesn't always give us what we want."

Erick grew silent, his weakness and fever compelling him to start again for his bedroom. Then he turned back again to his mother and brother and said, "Otto, I don't know if you are right on this or not. I just can't seem to let go. Still, I beg you, forgive me."

"All is forgiven," Otto assured him.

"There's nothing to forgive," said Ingrid. "You acted rashly but not really improperly. Mr. Withers was the real offender. What an unpleasant man! Now, back to bed with you; we'll talk more of this matter when you're feeling better."

Erick did as he was told.

Otto wasn't in the mood to talk, so Ingrid

went to the kitchen and started cleaning up. Her kitchen never had a chance to get dirty. Ingrid cleaned it every day and then cleaned it again. Even so, she always felt better when clanging things around in her kitchen, re-arranging the pans in the cupboard. The clunking and banging somehow always had a serene effect on her. So she arranged the pans loudly— and again, loudly.

Ingrid and Isabel visited regularly at church and two or three times a week on the phone, so she knew Ingrid would be surprised to see her come hurriedly through the door of the coal-yard office on Thursday morning.

"Hello, Ingrid! I have some wonderful news! At least it seems wonderful to me."

"Well, whatever is it?" Ingrid asked, raising her voice to match Isabel's obvious excitement.

"Otto wants to marry me!"

"This is news? That must be the oldest of news. Still, old or not, it's good news for everyone!"

"Are you sure, Ingrid? I know I wouldn't be marrying just Otto. And he wouldn't be marrying just me. He will be marrying into my past, my future, my Dizzy Izzy reputation. Are you ready to stick the McCaslin reputation into the Mueller family?"

"Isabel, for two generations now your people have called mine the 'coal people' and mine have called yours the 'cow people.' I'd say this isn't exactly the Hatfields and the McCoys trying to work something out with the Astors. But in God's good providence I see no reason why the coal people and the cow people shouldn't get together and try to find a little happiness."

Isabel laughed. "When I look around me, I can see that God must have given me the Muellers to help me sort things out. I love Otto. He must have inherited your total freedom from all biases. Still, times are hard. Otto was lamenting the fact that he didn't have the money to buy me an engagement ring."

The conversation ceased, and Ingrid sat still. Her eyes began to shelter tears at their corners. Isabel knew that Ingrid didn't mind tears; she considered them to be a sign of life. When she had sat and thought for a long time, Ingrid appeared to be in some kind of trance.

"What is it, Ingrid?" said Isabel. "You seem to be on another planet."

Ingrid looked up at Isabel and shook her head and smiled. Then they both burst out laughing, Ingrid to the point of tears. "Oh, Isabel, it feels good to laugh. Since Hans's death, I've done too little of it." She took a handkerchief from a desk drawer and dried the tears that had started in a fit of melancholy and flowed freely in laughter. She then grew serious again as she reached in Isabel's direction. "Let me see your hand." Isabel gladly extended her hand. Ingrid studied it and then studied her own. "My, your hands are strong, Isabel."

"You mean thick and muscular. We milk-maids get these fat fingers by squeezing the underside of a thousand cows. But just look at your hands—you're such a lady. You've got the kind of hands they photograph for cold-cream commercials to put in ladies' magazines."

"Yes, but you've got good hands. I don't know of anyone who uses them better. There's an old Bavarian proverb that says, 'Hands are what God gives us to serve His world, because He hasn't any himself.' So your hands are as noble as anyone else's. The only thing wrong with them is that they suffer from a want of jewelry."

Ingrid dropped Isabel's hand and then with her own right hand she pulled her old engagement ring off her left hand. It slid easily off of Ingrid's willowy hand. She took it and slid it onto the third finger of Isabel's hand. It went on perfectly—as if it had been fitted by a jeweler. It overwhelmed Isabel that it would even fit her finger.

Isabel was taken by the beauty of the ring,

which to her was a sparkling contradiction that a milkmaid should have such a beautiful object on her stubby, heavy hand. But the ring in coming to rest there performed a kind of miracle. Even to Isabel, her fingers seemed to elongate and all at once appear graceful, feminine.

"I'm one lucky woman," said Isabel. "No, I'm not lucky, I'm blessed. God has taken a liking to me for reasons I could never guess. And I am about to marry the world's greatest poet and have a mother again. Know what I think, Ingrid? I think God looked down and saw me milking our cows and said, 'There's my little Isabel. I'm going to pour so much wonder into her life that those around her will have to admit that nothing happens by accident.'"

"So true," agreed Ingrid. "Now give me back the ring and I'll give it to Otto. It's his place to present it to you."

"You're so right, and thank you!" Isabel pulled the ring off her finger and handed it to Ingrid, who slipped the ring back on her own hand.

"Would Thanksgiving be too early?" asked Isabel. "I haven't the foggiest idea where we'll live. Maybe we can arrange to buy the Witherses' old place. I understand it's going to be put up for sale."

"No, Isabel! Please, promise me you won't do that. You mustn't!"

Isabel was stunned by Ingrid's depth of feeling.

"Do you promise?" Ingrid insisted.

"Yes, of course. But why such strong feelings on the subject?"

"You know that Erick is in love with Mary. Well, I've lately come to see that the situation is not as hopeless as he thinks. Mary is not happy with Ted, but she doesn't feel free to leave him. In fact, I believe she's afraid to leave him. What scares me is that she might be threatened or cajoled into a marriage she knows isn't best—"

"Maybe," said Isabel, interrupting her, "she was so much in love with his brother Tom that she entered into this relationship all confused, remembering how good it was with Tom yet still not knowing what she wants. But do you really think she's with Ted against her will?"

"I do," said Ingrid in a bold manner. "Ted walked back into her life at a time when she was extremely vulnerable. She was contemplating a union with Erick, and then when she saw Ted, something changed with her."

Isabel suddenly became reflective. "And since Tom and Ted are identical twins, you can see how such a thing might happen. Hard to believe that what Mary found so good in Tom would turn out to be evil in Ted. They say that identical twins are identical in every way. One of them cannot be a prince and the other an ogre."

"I think it's more like Tom was Dr. Jekyll and Ted is Mr. Hyde," Ingrid said. "One was generous and kind, the other a werewolf by moonlight."

Isabel felt uncomfortable with Ingrid's interpretation. "Maybe, but Erick may have to let this one go. When Benny left me the first time, I was sure I had no reason to live. Only with a little perspective did I begin to see that his leaving was the best thing that ever happened to me. I thought I knew what was best, but I didn't."

"Do you compare Benny Baxter with Mary Withers?"

"No. A thousand times, no! The only thing that's similar is that we are sometimes forced to live with what has to be until we can see what should be." Isabel wasn't willing to talk any more about why she thought Ted was compelling Mary to leave Erick and even her home. "Ingrid, would you mind if I changed the subject a tad? I want to ask your opinion on a matter."

"Of course, Isabel, but promise me you'll pray for Mary. Let the happiness that you feel for Otto cause you to pray for Erick. If I'm wrong about Erick and Mary, I assure you I'll learn to accept it in time."

"I will pray. I promise you."

"What will you pray? Will you pray that Mary might find release and a way out of her confusion and misplaced love?"

"Well ... yes. Yes, I will. But I'll also pray that if Erick and Mary are not to be, that Erick will accept that."

It wasn't the kind of resolution either woman would have liked.

"Now, Ingrid," said Isabel, "here's what I want to ask your opinion about. It appears that Christine Cartwright is pregnant by Benny Baxter. You had already heard that, hadn't you?"

Ingrid nodded.

"Well, Benny sent me some money recently to help Christine with the baby. In his letter he denied that he's the child's father."

"Why did he send *you* the money?"

"He trusts me, I guess. He wants to be sure that Christine has enough to bring the baby into the world when the time comes. The problem is, I spent his money at the county hospital so they would admit Helena Pitovsky for the care she needed."

"Yes, Otto told me she was back in the hospital."

"Her life is hanging by a thread, I'm afraid."

"Poor woman, I pray that she lives. Whatever would her husband do without her? And the children . . ."

"Believe me, I've thought all of that over. So far, she isn't responding to treatment, and while I've tried to help Ernest with his family's problems, I can't imagine how I will be able to help him with something as big as this."

"How much money did Benny send?" Ingrid asked.

"Forty dollars."

"Forty dollars." Ingrid acted calm as she repeated the sum. "Well, times are hard but there must be some way to get Benny's forty dollars into Christine's hands like he intended."

"Do you think I did right to spend the money on Helena?"

"Probably not. I don't know. But Christine doesn't really need it yet, so there's no point in letting it lie around useless when somebody else does need it, and desperately."

Isabel stood and walked over to Ingrid and kissed her, then turned and walked to the door. She put her hand on the knob, looked back, and smiled. "That's exactly how I felt. Thank you, Ingrid. As usual, you've been a big help." She stepped out then and was gone.

The rest of the day was uneventful for Ingrid. Only two coal orders came in for the entire day. But the weather was warm still. Soon, when everything turned colder and that first frost showed up, the coal orders would begin increasing. She closed the office by turning over the *Open* sign that hung in the front window, displaying the word *Closed* on its back.

Otto had made the two coal deliveries to the west of town. Ingrid had no idea where he had spent most of the day. Probably at the library. His library time was sure to be severely cut back once the cold weather set in.

Arriving home, Ingrid pulled down the lid to the mailbox and found but a single letter inside. She gasped a little, for she recognized the handwriting. It was from Mary Withers and addressed to her. Ingrid was firm with her impulses, and her first one was to rip open the letter to see what Mary had to say. Yet she feared what it was she might say, so she rebuked her impatience and carried the letter into the house unopened and laid it on the table. Only after she had brewed some tea and put potatoes in the oven for dinner did she at last pour herself a cup and sit down in her favorite chair with the letter back in her hand.

Finally she tore the end off the envelope in tiny dainty rips to protect the letter inside from getting damaged. She pulled out the sheets, then flexed the fold fully open. There was a ceremony involved in opening important mail, for Ingrid knew Mary hadn't written her just to ask about the weather.

Dearest Ingrid,

I could wish myself well enough to write in a casual manner and chat about casual things, but the seriousness of my troubles forbids it. How I wish I could talk with you face to face. You have been a friend whose counsel and wisdom come from experience, and so I look to you once again for help.

I deeply apologize for the scene we caused the other day. It was wrong of us to stop by. I'm so sorry about Erick's illness. He is a wonderful man, and I trust by now he is back on his feet. I must also apologize for Ted's behavior. He embarrassed me with his brusque departure and above all his treatment of you and your family.

It is partly the bruises you saw on Alexis that have caused me to write this letter. But let me begin my plea for understanding in a more general way. I, who am always in need, have had to face needs that go far beyond the financial. Alexis has been well and for that I am most grateful to our heavenly Father. Still, I have grave concerns for her which derive from our new circumstances. Ted feels sure that our marriage must come soon. He assures me he loves me and that there has never been another for whom he has felt so deeply. And he insists that his love runs deep for Tom and believes that the book of Genesis teaches he is obligated to raise up a son for his dead brother. He grows daily in his insistence that we marry so we can have a son.

He is so pushy in this that I fear him. So far he has not struck me, but he has warned me twice, when he was angry, that if he cannot marry me, then no one ever will. If you could hear him when he says such things, I know you would understand my concern and fear.

The bruises on Alexis come from his continual rough treatment of her. He doesn't realize how strong he is. I try to tell him that he's hurting her, but he says I'm just exaggerating things. Alexis cowers before him each time he enters the room, and he resents her for not letting him hold her. It's easy to see she is terrified of him.

Sometimes I think I see signs of his softening up. I pray this will happen soon. I am tortured. If he knew I wrote this letter, he would be furious. He wants me to cut off all prior relationships with everyone I've ever known. I dare not call you for fear that the telephone bill would show me guilty of "clinging to the past," as he puts it. I beg you, please don't write back. If he should get to the mailbox before I did and find a letter from home, he would get very angry.

Oh, Ingrid, I thought I loved him. But if I really loved him, would I be this afraid? Please *pray for both Alexis and me. I hope to contrive a reason to return to King of Prussia before too long. I hope that when I do, we will be able to have a long talk. Ted wants us to be married in December. I'm afraid to commit to that date. Help me!*

Sincerely,
Mary Withers

The letter ended abruptly, as though Ted's sudden arrival had forced her into writing a premature conclusion.

Ingrid felt the pain of living between Mary and her son. What should she do? When she was younger, Ingrid had been friends with a woman who married an attractive but overbearing man. After the woman's children left home, she had lost her mind and was never able to live without assistance again.

Ingrid was afraid for Mary and Alexis. She must find a way to help them. She must.

This is too heavy for me, Lord, she prayed. *Please, show me you're close by. Help me to help Mary somehow, and don't let me go through this alone.* Ingrid folded Mary's letter and slid it back in the envelope just as she heard Otto coming through the front door.

Otto grinned.

Things were not so dark.

For certain needy souls the counter at the coal office was for them a place to come to find warmth. Hans hadn't been so easily swayed by the poor who walked in begging for coal. Ingrid, on the other hand, so enjoyed feeling warm that to her it seemed unfair to let people go cold just because they didn't have any money. As Ingrid reflected on these thoughts, Christine Cartwright burst through the office door of Mueller Coal Yard.

"Mrs. Mueller, the mornings are getting chilly, and my mother and I are cold right along with them." Christine didn't bother with hello or how are you. "I know I'm not well thought of in this town, but that doesn't mean I deserve to freeze to death."

"Whoa, slow down there, Miss Cartwright. We haven't even said our hellos yet. I assume what you're saying is, 'Give me some coal.'"

Christine shifted uneasily on her feet. She looked at Ingrid, then looked away. She twisted her handkerchief around her cold white knuckles, looked at Ingrid again, and then broke into tears. She sobbed so violently that Ingrid wished she would quit it. When she didn't, Ingrid walked around from behind the counter of the desk and placed her arm around Christine's shoulders.

"Have yourself a good cry, dear. Sometimes it's what we have to do to put our world back together," said Ingrid.

Just Ingrid's touch caused Christine to lose control all over again. A few moments later, she took a deep breath and said, "Mrs. Mueller . . . do you know how long it's been since anyone in this town has touched me or said a kind word to me?"

Ingrid stood silent.

"Well, I can tell you it's been quite a while. I wouldn't even be here except I have nowhere else to go. I know you know how I once lived in the city. I'm not proud of how I made my living. But I'm too old now to make a living like that. The younger ones are prettier than I and they take the customers who used to come to me. I'm so ashamed. . . ." Once more Christine started sobbing, and each time she erupted into tears, Ingrid felt all the more helpless.

"Chris," Ingrid said, "things can't be as bleak as all that." Ingrid couldn't imagine why she had called her Chris. It was too intimate, too friendly, given their relationship. But her use of the shortened first name, as if they were good friends, had awakened in Christine a further volley of tears.

"Thank you so much for calling me Chris," she said, sniffling and wiping her red nose.

"Isn't that your name? You can call me Ingrid if you like."

"It wouldn't be fittin', Mrs. Mueller."

"Nonsense. Referring to each other by our first names is a gift we give each other when we've decided formality is too stiff a way to go on with life. Perhaps it's not a great gift; it won't buy you coal or anything. But it's a gift all the same. So, I'm Ingrid, you're Chris. Is that clear?"

Christine nodded that it was. "Times are hard, Ingrid. No. Times are desperate. I can't find work, and people around here treat me like a leper."

Ingrid hardly knew what to say. It was clear that Christine was used to living alone and needed so badly to talk to someone that she would talk to anyone. The pressure of all she carried was like a bomb set to go off at any moment. Apparently Ingrid's touch had been the thing that detonated Christine's confession, her losing control here in the coal-yard office.

"When's the baby due?" Ingrid asked.

"You know about that too? I guess the whole town's talking about it already."

"Yes, dear, I guess news does travel fast around here."

"It's due in May." Christine wiped her eyes and continued. "What am I gonna do? Mama's mind is gone now. I shouldn't have left her to come here, but I've got to have some coal. We're so cold in the mornings. Ingrid, please . . ." Christine began sobbing all over again.

This time tears welled up in Ingrid's eyes as well.

"And I'm scared about the future, the baby coming. I can't expect Benny to acknowledge the child as his." Christine paused with a worried—perhaps questioning—look on her face. Ingrid showed no surprise. The word was out all over town; everyone had been informed by the gossip circles that she carried the Bible salesman's child. "I've got to find a way to pay the county for the delivery, even if that means having a doctor come to the house to deliver it. But that's a problem I'll deal with later. For now the old house isn't warm enough for Mama and me to stay well. In her current mental condition, if she were to get really sick, the additional care would be too much for us. I pray that each day things will get a little better, but God seems out to lunch. Every morning when I get up, everything just gets worse, not better, and I—"

Ingrid reached out with both her hands and gently took Christine's hands into hers, and immediately Christine stopped talking. "Christine, do you know the Twenty-third Psalm?"

"No, Mrs. Mueller."

"Ah-ah-ah," said Ingrid, wagging her finger. "What was our gift for the day?"

"I mean, no, Ingrid."

"Well, it's in the *Three Generation Regal Heritage Bible*. Do you still have one of those?"

Christine nodded. "I don't look at that Bible very much. Partly because I don't understand the Bible and partly because Benny sold it to me."

"It's a good Bible, Chris. Benny didn't write it, remember. God did, and you mustn't feel that it isn't God's Word just because the one who sold it to you didn't behave like the author. Anyway, the first line of the psalm says, 'The Lord is my shepherd; I shall not want.' Tell me, do you believe that?"

"Well, no ... maybe ... I don't really know. When I walked into the house a couple weeks ago I found that someone had brought over flour and potatoes. There was no note, no acknowledgment—they were just there in the kitchen. I have no idea who sent them, but I'm grateful for the gift."

"There you go!" said Ingrid. "Psalm Twenty-three in action. I don't know who gave you the groceries, but ultimately they came from God. The book of James says that every good and every perfect gift is from above, comes down from the Father of lights. So no matter which human source provided for you, you may be sure it was all the gift of God."

"I wish I could see that as clearly as you do," said Christine.

"God is about to give you another gift. I'm going to have Otto bring you a quarter ton of coal this afternoon. And I want no credit for this. The coal was God's long before they hauled it out of the mountains. It's His even as it lies out in our coal yard. I'm just one of His stewards. Besides, it's God's will that nobody ever be cold or hungry, no matter their past or their reputation."

"Mrs. Mueller—"

"Ah-ah-ah."

"Ingrid. I'm so grateful. Whoever owns the coal, you've managed to give it to me in a way that keeps me from feeling like a beggar. Maybe that's the best gift of the day."

Ingrid smiled. She liked her. As Ingrid tried to see her through the eyes of God, she realized Christine was pretty much like herself. She got cold and hungry and needed friends just like any of the good Lutheran women from the missionary sewing circle. "Christine," said Ingrid, "I'm thinking that eventually you're going to need more than a quarter ton of coal. And even though it's God's coal, I do have to pay for it. Most of the people I buy it from don't see it as God's coal, so they are often prompt and ruthless in sending me the bill for it. I'm going to ask you to pay for the second load I send you by helping me out here in the office. We're about to get into our busy season, and I don't want to be down here all by myself every day. I wonder—" Ingrid stopped for a moment and Christine remained silent. Then she said, "Come back here behind the counter with me."

Christine obeyed and seemed eager to hear what Ingrid had to say. Ingrid led her about fifteen feet to a door that opened into a small room. Inside were a chair and a cot.

"This little room is one we furnished for Hans so that he would have a place near the office to lie down when his back pain got real bad. It would be a good place for your mother to stay while you manage the front desk on your workdays. There's only one way in or out of this room, so she wouldn't be able to leave without your seeing her."

"My workdays?"

"Yes, I'd like it if you would come here every Tuesday and Thursday and help me out. I know you're pregnant, but you could sit here behind the desk between customers so your feet wouldn't swell. With you working here a couple days a week, I'd have a chance to catch up with my household chores and be a better grand-mother to Marguerite. Well, what do you think?"

"You mean you're giving me a job?"

"Yes, I guess that's what I mean."

Christine threw her arms around Ingrid, thanked her again and again, and assured her that she would be showing up at the coal-yard office promptly at eight o'clock on Thursday morning.

When she had left, Ingrid phoned Isabel.

"Isabel, could you stop and see me? Will you be in town today?"

"I'm on my way now," Isabel replied. "Helena is doing a little better and may even come home tomorrow. I need to pick up a few things to cook dinner for the Pitovsky family. Helena once confessed to me that she loves olives, so I'm going to splurge and buy her a homecoming bottle of olives." The phone line crackled and suddenly went silent, then came back alive. "I'm sorry about our phone, Ingrid. I told Peter it needs to be repaired but he hasn't gotten around to it. Now, what was it you wanted to . . ."

The line crackled again, followed by silence.

Though their conversation had been cut off, Ingrid had heard enough to know that Isabel was on her way over. Within fifteen minutes she was sitting in one of the two maple chairs in the front of the coal office. Ingrid sat in the other and they leaned toward each other.

"I had a visitor this morning," said Ingrid.

"Who?"

"Christine Cartwright. Her visit today has forced me to ask myself who owns what in life. Now I must ask you a question, Isabel. Who owns the McCaslin Dairy?"

"Peter and I do."

"Not God."

"I think I see what you're hinting at. You'd like for me to say that God owns the dairy?"

"Nobody knows better than you about how God owns the cattle on a thousand hills. So doesn't that mean He owns the McCaslin cows as well?"

"Well, God can certainly have my half of the cows. I don't mind. But I can't speak for my brother's half. I doubt, though, he would agree with you about the ownership of the dairy farm and the cows. Whatever has brought up this whole issue, anyway?"

"You know that forty dollars Benny sent you to give to Christine, which you turned around and used to pay Helena's hospital bill?"

"Of course. Why?"

"I may have figured out a way for you to gain back that money before Christine has her baby. In the meantime, Christine needs milk— two or three glasses a day while the baby's being formed. That's where you come in. Maybe you could take some milk from the dairy and make sure Christine and her mother get a little every day?"

"It's such a small amount, I could probably do it without my brother even knowing. In fact, I'll bring her a few bottles later today. What are you doing to help Christine?"

"I'm giving her some of God's coal. She's also going to be working for me here at the coal office every Tuesday and Thursday, at least until she gets close to the time of the delivery. I was wondering, is there anything she could do out at the dairy—just part time, mind you—to help her along? She won't be able to come to work without bringing her mother. She dares not leave Mabel alone anymore. One more thing—Christine will need to sit down from time to time while she's working."

"To be honest," said Isabel, "Monday mornings I'm so busy with the stores opening back up after the weekend run on the dairy cases, I could use Christine to wash and sterilize bottles, and she could run the bottlebrush sitting down. Her mother could sit and watch, I guess."

"That sounds perfect."

"Maybe, but Peter might not think so. He still holds it against me for when I hired Ernest. But Ernest was brought on as a full-time worker, including providing his family with a place to live. So it would be quite a bit different with Christine, with her just helping out on Mondays. I think Peter might be able to adjust to that."

"Thank you, Isabel."

"Don't mention it. But why the sudden interest in Christine's welfare?"

"Because God taught me a very important lesson this morning."

"Which was?"

"It reminded me of something Don Quixote said—that 'we are all the children of God.'"

"I guess even Christine Cartwright fits that description."

"And maybe you and I can help her to feel

like one of God's children. I promise to keep her warm if you promise to keep her and her baby healthy."

"I'll do the best I can," agreed Isabel.

Otto picked out a ring box. The jeweler, Mr. Jacobsen, offered to give it to him, but Otto insisted on paying for it.

"But why would you want to pay two dollars?" asked Mr. Jacobsen.

"Have you ever been in love, Mr. Jacobsen?"

The jeweler cleared his throat. "I guess ... sure ... why?"

Taking his mother's engagement ring from his pocket, Otto carefully placed it into the slot inside the small velvet box. "Because nothing this precious should be given without a cost. My mother wore this ring for years. Now that Papa is gone, this ring, which has proved the steadfastness of love, should at least come in a box that I paid for with my own money."

"Do you plan to become engaged today?" asked Mr. Jacobsen.

"Today!" Otto exulted.

"Can I get a closer look at the ring?"

"Of course," said Otto. He pulled the ring from the box and handed it to the jeweler.

Jacobsen turned the gold band in his hand and studied the inside. As he continued looking at it, he said, "There's nothing written on the inside of the ring—would you like me to inscribe the date of your engagement?"

"Yes, that's a great idea!"

"I'll do it and it won't cost you a penny."

"Then I don't want you to do it. Nothing must be free or cheap about this day!"

"Okay, okay. How about three dollars for the inscription of the date?"

"Fine, and could you also put *Song of Solomon 8:7* next to the date?"

"Whoa now. There's only so much room."

"Just abbreviate it, then. To *Cant. 8:7*. Can you do that?"

"Sure. That'll work."

"How much more?"

"How does another dollar sound?"

"That's fine. And thank you!"

Before driving out to the dairy, Otto stopped at home to pick up Marguerite.

"Now, Marguerite," said Otto, "when Daddy gets down on one of his knees to ask Isabel,

'Will you be my wife?' what are you going to do?"

"I'll get down on one knee too, and say, 'Will you be my mother?'"

"That's right! Very good!"

"Papa, is Miss Isabel marrying both of us?"

"Yes. In a way she is."

"What if she doesn't want to marry me? What if she only wants to marry you ... would you still marry her?"

"She does want to marry both of us."

"But if she says she'll marry you but not me, will you still marry her?"

It was a loaded question that Otto knew deserved a good answer. "Marguerite, I could never marry anyone who wouldn't agree to marry you also."

Marguerite hugged his neck and said, "I'm glad we're getting married 'cause I can't hardly remember my real mama anymore. Papa, who did you love more—my real mama or Miss Isabel?"

"Well, it's like this. When your mother was sick and I saw her getting sicker, I would sometimes get sick myself. I loved her so much, I didn't want her to be in any pain. I asked God not to take her home to heaven, because I truly thought I couldn't live without her. Then your mama made me promise that I would take care of you."

"And did you promise?"

"I sure did!"

"And are you sorry you kept the promise?"

"Never, not even for a minute." By this time it was beginning to get dark. Otto pointed at the sky and said, "Marguerite, do you see that star up there, that very bright star?"

"Yes, Papa."

"Well, that's not really a star. It's a planet; it's called Venus. Only we sometimes call it the evening star because it's the very first one you see after the sun has gone down. In just a moment it will be joined by a whole bunch of other stars, and although I don't know for sure where heaven is, I think maybe it's just out there beyond those stars and that your mother is looking down from there and she's smiling. She's smiling because she sees how much we love each other.

"But one night I looked up and I thought I saw her frowning, and I figured it was because she knew I was planning to marry Isabel. I thought I heard her say, 'Otto, my love, you be very sure that Isabel wants to marry Marguerite as well as you.' I told her, 'Renee, you don't have to worry, for Marguerite and I come as a package. Isabel either gets both of us or neither of us.' Then all those stars up there started twinkling and dancing, and your mama was smiling again."

"Papa, I love you! I think you and me and Isabel are going to have a very fine marriage."

After dinner Otto and Marguerite set out for the McCaslin place. The old coal truck had made many runs in that direction. But this was a special day. Otto had attached sunflowers to the truck's front grille and old Christmas ribbons to both side mirrors. He had painted eyelashes on the headlights and strung a banner across the front bumper that read, "They do not love that do not show their love," from Shakespeare's *Two Gentlemen of Verona*.

When they rattled into the front yard of the farmhouse, Isabel bounded exuberantly out the front door and doubled over with laughter on seeing the truck decorated so festively. She laughed out Juliet's words, " 'How camest thou hither, tell me, and wherefore?' "

Otto shouted Romeo's response. " 'With love's light wings did I o'er-perch these walls.' "

"And who is this?"

"This is the lady Marguerite. We've come together on a mission of some importance."

A few moments later they were all together in the parlor.

"Your truck speaks of something yet undone," said Isabel.

Immediately Otto dropped to one knee and looked up at Isabel. "Isabel, will you marry me?"

"Yes," said Marguerite, also kneeling. "And will you marry me too?"

Isabel drew Otto back to his feet and they kissed. He then handed her the ring box, and she opened it. Otto took the ring and slid it onto her finger. "Gladly!" said Isabel. "Most gladly will I marry you."

They embraced again, then both looked down at Marguerite, who was still kneeling. Otto and Isabel knelt down facing her, and Isabel said, "Marguerite, I will gladly marry you too. But wait a minute, something's missing. What could it be? Wait right here!"

Isabel hurried off to her bedroom and then just as quickly returned. She held in her hand a small satin box. "This is for you, Marguerite," Isabel said and gave it to her. The little girl's eyes grew wide with excitement. She opened the box. Inside was a tiny gold ring. Isabel said, "Marguerite, this gold ring is for you. I want the whole world to know that you and I are engaged to be married too. You can wear this ring, and when anybody asks you what it's for, you just tell them plainly that we're all three getting married."

"Isabel, I love you! Can I call you Mommy?"

"Of course you can. Coming from you, that's the most beautiful word I've ever heard."

They talked about many things over the next couple of love-filled hours. It would have been hard to tell who was proudest of her ring, Isabel or Marguerite. Otto felt like a complete person. In Isabel's presence he completely forgot he was crippled.

On the way out of the house that night, Otto handed Isabel an envelope. "Read this later," said Otto. "It's a testament of my love." Then he kissed her good-bye, and she kissed Marguerite good-bye, and he and Marguerite started for home.

Soon Isabel was alone in her room, where she sat down on her bed, opened the envelope, and let her eyes fall on the delicately inked page.

> *Thrice loved!*
> *First by a mother who lost me in the Great War,*
> *Second by a woman who lost me in her haste*
> *To gain the wider lands of immortality.*
> *Finally by a woman whose love of life*
>   *is something to be kept.*
> *Do I have imperfections? Every mirror says so.*

Yet these three loved never saw them.
I hobble, yet these believe I run.
I am afraid of all darkness, yet these three tell me
*   I am brave.*
I am penniless, yet all of these say I have made
*   them rich.*
Come, love, let us build a great cathedral and
*   name it love.*
Let our intentions be the heavy stones of that
*   foundation.*
Let our promises be mortar for the enduring
*   stone.*
Let our touching in the night be the soaring arches
*   of our confidence.*
Let the daily rehearsals of all our promises
Be the buttresses that keep the walls in place.
Let our love of God be towering colored windows
Where the rainbows of eternity gather sunlight for
*   our darker times.*
Above the altar of our love
Will be a crucifix to remind us
That marriage, like the life of our redeeming
*   Lord,*
Must have its Calvary.
We shall let the dying Jesus teach us that
Unless we're willing to die for each other,
We will never really live for anything worthwhile.
Our communion cup will be a simple gourd,
Cut like a dipper from which each of us will
Serve the other water
And hold it as our best communion.

Then shall we know simplicity
And treasure ordinary things,
And kiss and hope and worship God and live.
And when we come at last to that final service of
*   our love,*
We shall hang our faith on the bell ropes to set
*   the carillons ringing,*
And all the world shall know
That angels keep the Eden we establish.

Isabel was silent. To her, Otto was a kind of brilliance, though one that was unaware of its shining. Or like the desert rain that's oblivious to how it makes the flowers blossom. How much she owed her limping Adonis, who had come home wounded from the war, ready to face the greater war of life.

It had been a heady day indeed, and her eyelids beckoned for Isabel to sleep now. She felt the need to give herself to dreams that grew from the wondrous events of the day. Yet she lay awake a long time. Euphoria kept her alert, prevented her from falling asleep. And so she blessed the joy, knowing that to be kept awake by joy is itself a joy.

8

What is she doing here?"

"I hired her." It was a rehearsal of an old theme, an old argument Isabel had going with her brother, Peter.

"Hired her to do what?"

"Peter, you know very well that Mondays are a hard day around here. All our accounts come due, and the dairy cases at the stores need to be restocked. I thought this one day a week I could use a little help, that's all."

Peter's eyes flashed fire, then he decided to give in, even though he cared nothing for Christine. It was critical that Isabel remain ignorant of the unfinished shady business between Peter and Christine. She wouldn't guess at the secret they shared. She would never know about the attempted blackmailing that had gone on only a few months earlier. She would never hear about the old photo and the receipts and the infidelity that had made the McCaslins and the Cartwrights more one family than two.

Only after Isabel had taken the dairy truck to town to buy some groceries did Peter approach Christine. He appeared to be somewhat unnerved by Mabel, who sat in the corner twisting her dress around her knuckles, sometimes nearly to the point of immodesty. But Mabel wouldn't have understood that her presence bothered Peter. It was clear that she and her mind were so far parted they rarely kept company.

When the growl of the dairy truck faded, Peter told Christine, "I'm willing to let you work here, but I have to warn you against ever telling Isabel about how we're all sort of related. She doesn't know about it, and that's the way I want it to stay. Do you understand me?"

Christine nodded. She wasn't going to say anything, but then as Peter was about to turn and leave, she cleared her throat and said, "Mr. McCaslin, as you probably know, I've been reduced to poverty. I have no hope of making it except for what your sister and Mrs. Mueller—"

"The coal people?"

"Well, yes. But what I'm saying is, I'm not only reduced to poverty, I'm reduced also to the kind of powerlessness that has caused me to be honest. I know I was out of line when I gave you so much trouble last summer. I was brazen and heartless beyond words. The fact that we have the same father will never lure me again to use that against you. Since the robbery of our house in the summer, I've lost all proof that this was ever so. You owe me nothing. And any scorn you would show me would be too little for the hurt I tried to cause you. Please, let me keep this job, and all that has passed between us will remain silent forever."

"Do I have your word on that?"

"You do. I promise."

"All right then, thank you. Now, do be careful that you don't slip on the bottling room floor. The soap can make it slick at times."

"Thank you, Mr. McCaslin. I'll be careful."

Peter left and then Christine felt another surge of the grace of God. She would receive three dollars for each Monday she worked at the dairy, while Ingrid would pay her four dollars for her work on Tuesdays and Thursdays. She felt almost rich—to have enough milk and coal and to be able to earn seven dollars a week. Somehow she would make her life work.

Christine looked out the window of the

bottling room when she heard the old truck in the driveway. Crowded together in the truck with Isabel were Ernest and Helena Pitovsky. Christine wasn't quite through cleaning the milk bottles when Ernest walked into the bottling room.

"Hello, Miss Cartwright," he said. "Isabel told me you'd be working here on Mondays. I haven't been employed at the dairy for very long but I can tell you that you are sure welcome."

"Thank you, Ernest. There's something most special about Isabel, don't you think?"

"Yes, ma'am, I do. Me and my Helena were so far down on our luck when she found us. We were living in a junked car down by the railroad trestle. Because of her, we have a decent place to live and I have a job. And Helena, in spite of her setbacks, is getting stronger every day."

Christine's impression was that Ernest felt he had found more goodwill than he deserved. She understood such a thing. "Ernest, do you believe in God?"

"Well, as of late I sure do. I won't lie to you, though. I've had my doubts along the way. Sometimes when I see rich people, I wonder how they got it all and left so little for the rest of us. But I've learned that it's a sin to live in poverty and begrudge the rich. God exists wherever you look hard for Him. Six months ago I woke up every morning afraid I would lose my wife and my children would starve. Then, on one of the most ordinary days, Isabel came along. That's when I quit asking why if there's a God was I so poor. Instead, I told myself there must be a God, because one good woman for no good reason I could think of stopped to care. Then my Helena said, 'Ernest, there must be a God, because Isabel has His virtues, and God is the only one she could get those kind of virtues from.'"

"Ernest, I'm pregnant."

"Yes, I guess I've heard that." It was a blunt and unnecessary exchange of facts.

"A week ago I found myself penniless, not knowing what to do next. Since then, Ingrid and Isabel have helped me to look up. I've now got coal and milk and seven dollars a week. I'm going to church Sunday because I want to learn more about this whole thing called faith. Do you know what Psalm Twenty-three says?"

"Isn't that the one that says 'The Lord is my shepherd; I shall not want'?"

"That's the one. Is the Lord your shepherd?"

"Yes, ma'am."

"Are you in want?"

"No."

"I'm not in want either. I was standing at my

kitchen window just last night, thinking about how my reputation isn't all that great. Most people know I'm pregnant and probably figure there's not the slightest hope the baby's father will ever come forward and acknowledge us. So I made up my mind standing there looking out the window that if God will have me, I'll have Him. I made a deal with God that if He would forgive my waywardness, I'd look Him up in church."

"Sometimes, Miss Christine, I get the feeling that some of the people in the church wish I wasn't there. But then I remember that the church doesn't belong to them; it belongs to God, who loves us all the same."

"That's just how I feel about things. That if God wants me there, it doesn't much matter who doesn't."

Ernest grinned, said he had to get going, then turned and left the room.

Christine was about to start the long walk home with her mother when she heard Isabel shouting at her, "Just where do you think you're going?"

"Me and my mother must leave for home now. It feels like it could frost tonight."

"You're right—you are going home. But you're wrong if you think you're going to walk. I will drive you home on Mondays. You mustn't ever try to walk; it's too far into town. Especially as the days get shorter and colder. Do you promise me you won't try it?"

"I promise, Miss Isabel. And, again, thank you."

They were soon in the dairy truck and headed for Christine's home. It was several moments before Christine noticed the ring on Isabel's hand. "That's some rock you got there!" exclaimed Christine.

"Otto gave it to me! We're engaged now. I've never been happier."

Christine stared out the truck's window. "I'm so happy for you," she said, turning toward Isabel. "I could only wish that my child might have come into the world in such a way. You know, marriage first and children later. Miss Isabel, do you mind if I ask you a personal question?"

"Of course not."

"You knew Benny much longer than I did. Did he ever make you think that the good life was there for the asking?"

"I was younger then, but yes, he had a way of making me believe he held the keys to all things wonderful. I used to hope that one day Benny would come back for me and we'd live in a castle somewhere—wherever Benny had gone after he left here."

"Did you ever . . . with Benny, I mean. That is, did you—"

"If you're asking if I've ever *been* with Benny, the answer is no. For some reason he never pushed me into a compromising situation. I'm genuinely sorry, Christine. He was terribly wrong to take advantage of you in that manner."

"I wasn't exactly a virgin. Benny knew that, and he simply used me because in his mind it was a way to get what he wanted at no cost to himself. Still, I must say that more than he could guess, he has given me back a life I might never have had otherwise. Sometimes I feel the baby kicking and it's as if this little life is prodding me toward responsibility, or maturity. Up to now I've lived my thirty-five years thinking only of myself. Now my mother and my unborn child have wakened me to real life. I'm in charge of someone, and if I don't stand up to the charge, they won't make it. So, more than he ever knew, what happened with Benny has forced me to finally grow up. For that I'm grateful."

"Chris, your circumstances have made you look up. I'm engaged now, and that sense of God's goodness you feel touches me as well."

"My resources are an anonymous bag of groceries, coal and milk, and two part-time jobs.

But most of all, God. This Sunday I'm going to brave all the ugly gossip and attend services at the church. Will they welcome me, you think?"

"Not all of them. But remember, they don't own the church, my dear. That's God's house, and I guarantee you that He will be glad to see you."

Too soon the dairy truck pulled up to the Cartwright residence. Christine helped Mabel out of the truck and to the house and then turned and waved good-bye to Isabel before stepping inside.

During the trip back home, there were two things that haunted Isabel. First, she couldn't get out of her mind the odd looks she had seen pass between Peter and Christine that very morning. It had appeared that they held some heavy truth together. Or was she just being silly and imagining such a thing?

Of the other thing, however, she had no doubt. She had taken forty dollars of Christine's money. She must replace the money right away and then fess up to what she had done. The confessing part wouldn't be hard, but figuring out where to get the forty dollars would be.

Ingrid might know. Maybe together they could find a way to come up with the money, to get Benny's forty dollars back to Christine. In the meantime Isabel had an assignment. She would make sure she arrived at church early Sunday morning so that when Christine walked through the door, there would be someone besides God standing there to make her feel welcome.

She glanced at the diamond on her finger. It sparkled like the frost she was sure would come by morning.

She thought of Otto and remembered how much she owed.

Ahead of her the late afternoon sun was setting the sky ablaze as she drove on toward the dairy, toward the very heart of the solar flame. The fading sun coming through the truck's dusty windshield was as warm as the center of her soul. God had put her on Earth for a reason, which she knew had to do with counteracting the desperate shortage of love in the world.

The world was far from perfect. Ingrid carried a great loss with her husband's death. And Erick, the brother of her fiancé, who had recently recovered from the flu, was languishing from a lost dream. Erick's heartache was another reason Ingrid didn't laugh much anymore.

Isabel could see the dairy looming up ahead,

less than a mile away. The distance would be just enough time to remember Erick. "God, help Erick. If there's help enough in heaven, help Erick."

She realized this was only half the prayer she needed to pray. "And, God," she added, "there's Mary too. Help her not to make a mistake with Ted."

Isabel was through praying. For now. She rarely said amen but felt that open-ended prayers were the best kind, making it easier for her to pick up where she left off the next time she needed to speak with God.

Pulling the truck into the driveway, she saw through the window that Peter and his baby daughter, Elizabeth, were playing in the living room.

"There's a letter for you—right there on top of the stack," said Peter as a greeting.

"Thanks," responded Isabel as she found the letter and headed toward her bedroom. The sounds from the kitchen told her that Kathleen had started making supper.

It was another letter from Benny. Immediately she tore it open, and two more twenty-dollar bills fell out. The letter was yet another request for her to add this money to the previous forty dollars and to save them for the delivery of Christine's baby. This letter was different from the first, however. It contained a confession. Beginning with the third paragraph, the letter read, *I'm afraid I misled you in the letter before. The truth is that the child Christine carries is mine. I'm ashamed of taking advantage of Christine the way I did, and I must honestly say the only thing worse than denying the child is mine would be my failure to provide for it. Isabel, I must continue to implore you to help me in this matter of taking care of Christine's child, for as I said, it is my child too.*

Benny's forthright words surprised Isabel. Perhaps he had actually begun to read and believe the Good Book he'd spent his life selling to others. For some reason, Isabel wanted to believe that even Benny had a place in his heart for all that was honest and good.

Isabel hid the two twenties in a safe place and resolved that she would act honestly by quickly replacing the two that she had used to pay Helena's hospital bill. Detecting a wonderful aroma in the air, Isabel headed to the kitchen to help Kathleen.

Two hours later she climbed into bed and waited for the morning. Only God knew for sure what the morning would bring.

Suddenly cold, she pulled the covers up to her chin. "The frost will come tonight," she whispered absentmindedly. It was a phrase spoken into the darkness, swallowed up by the thin cold air above her bed.

When Ingrid got up on Tuesday morning, Isabel's prophecy—unknown to Ingrid—had come true. White covered the ground. The frost had come, a glorious frost. Now Pennsylvanians would pick the last of the apples, the kids would carve their jack-o'-lanterns.

It was the final week of October, and Erick had been back to work for three weeks now. His bout with the flu and Mary's surprise visit had taken a lot out of him, and while he was doing better now, he still looked a little peaked to Ingrid. Getting over the flu was easy. Getting over Mary was not.

Ingrid hadn't told him about Mary's letter. She was afraid he might see it as a reason to go to her and try to interfere. He was already convinced she was making a big mistake. Ingrid knew he was right in how he felt about Mary.

Mary's letter had confirmed the fact. Even so, Erick had a way of compounding Mary's mistakes, so Ingrid thought it wise he not know about the letter.

Marguerite was off to school by eight on this cold morning and Otto to the coal yard to load the truck. He had five deliveries to make. Ingrid felt glad that their oversupply of coal ordered for the previous unusually warm winter was now beginning to pay off. Christine would be running the desk at the coal office. All in all it was a wonderful morning to be by herself at home.

Ingrid made herself some tea. Though she preferred tea to coffee, the men in her life never had. She hadn't enjoyed many mornings of solitude since Hans's funeral, so when they came she camped out in the quietness of her soul and sometimes did strange things.

This particular morning she read the *New York Times*, Ingrid's favorite link to the world and cultures outside King of Prussia. The days since Hans's illness were long and weary and had required so much from her that she rarely finished her reading of the *Times* until Thursday. But on this casual day she was already down to the personals, a section of the paper she never missed. She was always moved by the pain and struggle that came packed into such few lines. Such as *Buddy, come home. I don't care if you play your music.* Or *Harold, Chi-Chi forgives you* or *Does anyone out there have a recipe for Nantucket squash pie?* or *Sonnie Lou, Momma's dying. Please call.*

Among these, Ingrid read, *Teddy dear, the children miss you. Please come home. Alicia Withers.* The notice wouldn't have roused much interest in Ingrid except that the address given was in Hereford, Pennsylvania—a town only about forty miles north. And the pet name *Teddy dear* was what Mary Withers had called Ted on that awful day they stopped by, when Erick had made such a scene. Last names were rarely used in personals, yet the last name of this Alicia was given, and it was Withers! So Alicia Withers and her *Teddy dear*, along with his questionable extended absence, became like snags in Ingrid's mind.

On a hunch Ingrid decided to answer the personal. *Dear Alicia, I may have information on Teddy dear. Inga Petrovalov, general delivery, King of Prussia, PA.*

Exactly a week later, with Christine taking care of things at the coal office, Ingrid visited the post office and asked the postmaster, "William, is there any mail for Inga Petrovalov?"

"Indeed there is. But, Ingrid, have you any proof that you are Inga?"

"Please, I'm using an alias and this is most important."

William winked. "You wouldn't be joining one of those widows' clubs, now would you?"

"No, I've not joined a club for widows!" Ingrid suddenly wished she had used the post office in a nearby town where she wasn't so well known. "Do I get the letter or not? I can assure you it's mine."

The postmaster winked again, which made Ingrid both nervous and angry. She took the letter from the grinning man and left the building. She opened it and saw nothing that would confirm or deny the true identity of Teddy dear. It simply read, *Dear Inga, if you know where Teddy is, please write me and include his address.*

Knowing she had to be more specific to speed things along, Ingrid went straight home and wrote a second letter. *Dear Alicia, did Teddy ever mention if he had a brother?* Then she walked to the funeral home and asked to see their old obituary photos. The director had one of Tom Withers, taken just before his untimely death more than five years before. Ingrid asked if she could borrow the photo, and the director told her that she could keep it.

"We usually don't keep pictures this old anyway," he said. "If you don't mind my asking, why the interest in Mary's dead husband?"

"I'll tell you later sometime. Sorry, but I have to go," said Ingrid, hurrying out of the mortuary. *Why do people have to be so nosy?* she thought as she walked. Of course, Ingrid had to admit that she was doing a great deal of nosing around herself. But her case was different; she was doing it for a very noble purpose. When she arrived back home, she enclosed the photo of Tom in her letter to Alicia Withers and added a final line that said, *Could the enclosed photo be a picture of Teddy dear?*

This time Ingrid didn't have to wait a week for a reply. Just four days later the postmaster phoned Ingrid at the coal-yard office. "Is this Inga Petrovalov?" he asked.

"Well . . . yes. Yes, it is!"

"I'm holding a letter for you, Ingrid—I mean, *Inga*."

What unnerved Ingrid was that William burst into laughter after he said the alias. Ingrid slammed the receiver down onto its cradle. She took out a piece of paper and wrote that she would be back soon, taped the note to the front window of the coal office, then locked the door and headed to the post office.

"Hello, Inga! Looks like you've got some mail." William winked at her and then turned to retrieve the letter. He was still chuckling when Ingrid left the post office. She walked directly back to the coal-yard office and was relieved to see there was no one waiting to see her. She pulled the letter from its envelope almost as soon as she opened the door.

> *Dear Inga,*
>
> *The photograph you sent is indeed my husband! Where did you get it? Do you know how I could get in touch with him? The children and I are very desperate. We haven't seen Teddy in over seven months. He left me right after I told him I was pregnant. My third child is due soon. I feel trapped. Please help me.*
>
>
>
> *Thank you,*
> *Alicia Withers*
>
>

Ingrid was stunned. This was the very answer she had hoped for but also feared. She lost no time in writing her next letter. *Dear Alicia, I'm most anxious to see you reunited with Teddy. I'll be getting in touch with you soon. Inga Petrovalov.* Ingrid mailed it and waited two days before asking Otto if he could drive her to Hereford early the next morning. Because the narrow roads were mostly unpaved, the trip took a good hour and a quarter. Ingrid acted all secretive on the matter, refusing to share with Otto her reasons for wanting to visit

Hereford. Otto would drive Ingrid anywhere she wanted to go, but he had to admit he was baffled by his mother's request to go on this journey.

Once they reached Hereford, Ingrid instructed Otto to park in front of the post office. Ingrid climbed down out of the coal truck, being careful to perform the awkward maneuver and still appear like a lady. She and Otto walked to the bench outside the post office and sat down. They had gotten there in time to see the nation's flag raised and the postmaster put out the fiber mat for people to wipe their boots on.

Now Otto started insisting that Ingrid tell him what was up and why they had made the long drive to Hereford so early in the morning.

Deciding it would be better to let him know a few things, Ingrid said, "You must help me watch the post office, Otto. I'm looking for a young woman, pregnant, perhaps with two children—I don't know. But any woman who comes to this post office asking for a general-delivery letter, I must talk to her. I have a feeling we won't have to wait long."

"But, Mama, you still haven't told me why in the world we're even in this town!"

He was right. "Otto, go wait in the truck. I mustn't appear to have company."

"Why?"

"Don't *why* me! Please, just do as I ask. I'll explain later. Now go back to the truck!"

Knowing the conversation was over, Otto obeyed. He stood and walked to the coal truck, shaking his head as he went. With Otto out of sight now, Ingrid kept her place on the bench.

Only fifteen minutes after the post office opened, Ingrid saw a very pregnant woman with two children enter the building. A few moments later, when the woman and children emerged from the building, the woman carrying a single letter in her hand, Ingrid jumped from the bench. "Alicia! Is that you? I am Inga Petrovalov!"

Otto, who had his window fully down, heard his mother's words and his mouth fell open. He shouted from the truck, "Inga Petrovalov? Mother—"

"Stay in the truck, Otto," Ingrid shouted back, cutting him off. "And don't say anything!"

"You . . . you are Inga?" the woman said.

"Yes, Alicia. It is I, Inga Petrovalov, the one who's been writing you."

Otto stared as the two women, followed by the children, walked over and sat on the bench. Ingrid glanced over her shoulder at her son, determining to share the story with him as soon as she was sure of her facts.

"So, Alicia, is it? Do I have that right?"

The woman nodded. She looked tired. "Yes, I'm Alicia Withers. I can't tell you how much I appreciate your helping me find Teddy. As you can see, my baby could come any time and I must have him home. I need him, Inga."

Suddenly Ingrid felt guilty about the alias. "Actually, my real name is Ingrid. And the photo I sent you is not of Ted Withers but of Tom, Ted's twin brother."

"What?" Obviously confused, the woman stared at Ingrid.

"But Tom has since passed away," said Ingrid. "He died five years ago and left his wife a widow. She's a good friend of mine. Didn't Ted, or Teddy, ever tell you he had a twin?"

"Yes, but he told me he died of whooping cough when he was a baby."

"I don't know how to tell you this, Alicia, but your boyfriend—"

"Teddy isn't my boyfriend." Alicia stiffened, then added, "He's my *husband*."

"You mean to say you were married to Teddy?"

"Not were, *am*!" she insisted. "We were married by a justice of the peace over in Allentown six years ago."

Ingrid's mouth dropped open. "You're married to him?"

"That's right. Teddy sold insurance and was always on the road. He was a good salesman too, at least until the hard times started. Then he took to the road more than ever and we hardly ever saw him. But this last time he's been gone so very long and hasn't kept in touch. I'm out of money. I must find him. The children and I"—she gestured toward her two children—"we need Teddy to come back home. I just hope he's all right."

For the first time Ingrid considered the children involved in all of this. When she did, she was struck with a deep sympathy for them. The children looked thin and pale, their clothes ragged. They played around the bench where the two women talked, understanding nothing of the weighty things being said.

"Have you seen my husband?" the woman asked.

"Yes ... quite recently. Here's his address," said Ingrid. She took a piece of paper from her purse and handed it to Alicia. "He's living on his mother's farm over in Albany."

"You must be mistaken! Teddy was raised in an orphanage in New York City. That's why I ran the personal in the *Times*. I thought he might be living back in New York and see the advertisement."

"No, Alicia." Ingrid chose her words carefully. "I'm sorry, dear, but I'm afraid you've been lied to. Ted was raised on his mother's farm with his twin brother, Tom. That's where he is even now."

Alicia looked like one coming out of a stupor. She shook her head as though it would somehow bring the world back into perspective, back to normal once again.

"I must ask you," said Ingrid, "and I hope I'm not presuming . . ."

"No. Please, go on." Alicia now had tears rolling down her cheeks, which, together with the painful expression on her face, gave her the look of a person profoundly wronged.

"So you and Ted never sought out getting a divorce?"

"Certainly not," Alicia replied, wiping her eyes. "Teddy doesn't believe in divorce. He says divorce is a convenience invented by people too lazy to work on their difficulties."

It was becoming quite apparent to Ingrid just how strongly Ted didn't believe in divorce; it appeared he was getting ready to be married to two women at once.

As Ingrid stood to leave, Alicia clutched in her hand the piece of paper with Ted's address on it. "Could I ask you one final question?" Ingrid asked.

The woman looked sullenly over at the children and nodded.

"Was Teddy ever mean or abusive to your children?"

The question proved to be too much, for Alicia then broke into sobs. Ingrid sat back down next to her on the bench and held her as she cried and shook.

When she had regained enough control of herself, she said, "He never meant to be that way to the children. He thought he was just correcting them so they would grow up decent. I always worried, though, that he would go too far and really hurt them. Once he slapped Tonia there so hard I couldn't take her to church for fear of people asking questions about the bruises."

Her words made Ingrid very afraid for Alexis. "My dear," she said, "if I were you, I would act on this very fast. I believe your Teddy has a great deal more money than you suspect, and I believe he intends to marry again soon."

"What? But he's married to me!"

"I assure you, his current fiancée will be just as surprised as you to find out what Ted has been up to here. You can trust me on this, Alicia. Ted is making plans to marry his brother's widow. Probably within the next month or two."

Alicia finally stood and gathered her children close to her. She was still weeping when Ingrid gave her a hug and left her standing there with the children looking up at their mother. Once Ingrid climbed inside the coal truck, she looked back and gave a little wave. Alicia's silhouette, which accentuated her very round shape, caused Ingrid to have to fight back tears.

"Let's go home, Otto," Ingrid said as she slammed the truck door shut.

Otto started up the truck and pulled out into the street toward home. "Mama, what was all that about?" he asked.

"That poor woman is the wife of Ted Withers. Those children are his."

Otto about drove off the road. "But how can that be? You mean she *was* Ted's wife?"

"No. She *is* his wife!"

"How did you find all this out, Mama?"

"The *Times*," she answered.

"What...?"

"I'll tell you that part later. Otto, for Erick's sake I'm glad all this happened. But that poor woman is shattered. Here she is about to give birth to Ted's third child and she's absolutely penniless. If she doesn't do something right away, there's a good chance Ted will go to jail for bigamy."

Ingrid knew that Erick would be relieved, even happy, when he found out the truth about Ted. It was obvious to everybody that his love for Mary was as strong as ever. She suspected that Mary and Alexis would be relieved to hear the news as well. Yet Mary would also be shattered but in a different way than Alicia. Not so much because she loved Ted. Ingrid could tell that Mary's early infatuation had faded. Instead, she would be crushed by her own foolishness and the way she allowed her late husband's memory to be superimposed onto his identical-looking brother, only to turn into something hurtful to her and Alexis.

The truck rattled and banged over a rutty section of road, calling Ingrid back from her musing.

"Otto, for now let's not tell anyone about our trip to Hereford and what we discovered."

"Not even Erick?"

"Especially not Erick."

"But won't he be angry with us when he finds out that we knew and kept it from him?"

"It's more likely he will be hurt than angry. It's just that I think he needs to come across this in his own way, in his own time. Maybe when the dust settles, it will be Mary herself who tells him. That would be the best way for him to find out. Even if Mary never returns to King of Prussia, we need to give Erick all the time and space he needs. Are we agreed?"

Otto turned and smiled. "Agreed. You know best."

Ingrid wasn't all that sure that she did know best. Deep down she wished she could have brought about the same result without interfering so much. When it came to the happiness of her family, she wasn't against interfering. But she decided that from now on she wanted to interfere only in good ways. Now that she had thoroughly interfered in Erick's affairs, she felt she ought to poke her nose just a bit into Otto's affairs.

The truck ran over a large pothole and pitched her forward in the seat, causing her almost to hit the windshield with her head. When she settled back again, it seemed a good time to ask, "Otto, have you and Isabel hit on a date for the wedding yet?"

"We were thinking about the second Sunday of Advent."

"That's a splendid idea. Marguerite would like that, since it's so close to Christmas."

"I think Marguerite actually thinks it is her wedding we're planning. She shows the ring Isabel gave her to everybody and says, 'Isabel and Daddy and me, all three of us are getting married!' "

Ingrid laughed. "That's what Alexis used to say when it looked as though Mary and Erick would marry. Otto?"

"Yes?"

"I was wondering . . . what do you think will happen when Alicia Withers and Mary Withers meet? I'd love to be a little mouse and—" Ingrid stopped and changed her mind about how she would finish the thought. "Of course, I'm not one to pry." She waited for Otto to argue with her.

She waited and waited.

The truck rattled on.

10

Nothing wakes her up?" asked Dr. Drummond.

"It seems no noise can rouse her," said Kathleen. "She's a happy child when she does wake up. In fact, she rarely cries. Peter, tell the doctor what happened last Saturday night."

"Well, I was playing with Elizabeth and teasing her. I don't remember what we were playing, maybe peekaboo or something like that. Anyway, she just went to sleep on me, just like that she went limp. It was the strangest thing. Doctor, I'm scared to death of this polio thing that's sweeping the country. This is how it starts, isn't it? Well, isn't it?"

"True, sometimes it can start like that," replied Drummond. "At least that's how my colleagues describe it. But not always. Please, let's not jump to conclusions. It could be lots of things. Polio is just one of them."

"Do you think it could be some kind of—" Peter hesitated, and his mouth could hardly form the words—"retardation or epilepsy?"

"I don't think so. Those usually carry some other symptoms she doesn't appear to have. Has she experienced any spasms or other uncontrollable movements?"

Peter shook his head. "You know the Denman girl came down with that infantile paralysis—polio? It's been all over upstate New York, and now it's here! They say she—the little Denman girl—just fell down and then couldn't get up. They've got her in an isolation ward over in Philly." Elizabeth was lying almost still now. "Look at her, Doctor. It isn't like she's not moving; it's more like she *can't* move." Peter shook his head. His fears sometimes drove him to near panic. A single tear welled out from one of his eyes, fell to his cheek and then to his shirt, which absorbed it.

Kathleen remained quiet, gently rubbing Elizabeth's arms and legs.

"Peter, I want you and Kathleen to take Elizabeth home. Meanwhile, I'll make arrangements to do some tests tomorrow."

"But tomorrow might be too late. What if she needs a doctor tonight? What if—"

"Like I said before, let's not jump to conclusions. She'll be all right staying with you until tomorrow. I'll meet you at the city hospital in the morning."

With Elizabeth in her mother's arms, Peter and Kathleen left the doctor's office and made their way home. The baby slept the entire way, then once at home she seemed to come alive again and for the next several hours was wide awake and played and laughed as usual.

She ate her farina and some mashed fruit, and drooled and enjoyed the meal with delight. At such moments she seemed healthy and normal, and Peter wondered if maybe his fear of Elizabeth getting polio was just that, a fear.

But then at nine-thirty that evening her joy was taken from her, and she grew eerily quiet. Elizabeth's little legs quit thrashing, her arms grew listless, and her smile disappeared. She fell instantly into a deep sleep, the kind of sleep that to Peter came too quickly and seemed too still.

"See there, Kathleen!" he said to his wife as she picked up the baby and carried her to her crib.

"See what?"

"Elizabeth—she's here one moment and gone the next!"

"She's worn herself out, that's all. She's tired."

"Open your eyes! She's not fallen asleep. She

sometimes leaves us ... but not of her own accord. She's taken from us by this thing ... this polio thing."

After Kathleen had laid the baby down, she and Peter collapsed against each other in tears. They agreed to take turns watching Elizabeth through the night to be sure she kept breathing. The idea behind their agreement was that while one stayed close by the crib watching the baby, the other would get some sleep. But neither of them could fall asleep, for their fears stalked them both all night long.

During one of Peter's turns to be with the baby, in the wee hours of the morning, he had a visitation. He was very tired by now and could in no way account for the strange rustling of the drapes, as if the window were open. Peter checked the baby. Her breathing was shallow but steady. He walked over and checked the window. It was shut tight.

He sank down to a sitting position with the hair raising up on the back of his neck. "Is someone there? Kathleen?" But Kathleen's long night of fatigue had at last conquered her, and she was too drowsy to hear him. She stirred in the next room and shifted on the mattress so that the old bedsprings creaked. Peter felt icy fingers grip him in the pit of his stomach. "Is someone there?" he repeated. Then he stood and wheeled around. But nothing—no stalker or prowler anywhere.

He smiled and told himself he was behaving foolishly. Then the light went out! Why? There was no electrical storm. Perhaps the light bulb had just burned out. He couldn't remember when he'd last replaced it. The darkness amplified his fear. It was so dark he could see nothing, although he thought he felt a heaviness in the room. He thought he heard the drapes swish, but he couldn't be sure. He turned in the darkness and knocked over an end table. It fell with a crash, spilling a saucer and teacup onto the hardwood floor. Peter himself had created the noise, yet the sudden roar of it had terrified him to the point that he uttered a small cry.

Kathleen stirred in their bed.

Dark angels come in the darkness. That's what his Scottish grandmother used to say. It was one of her superstitions. Still, Peter couldn't afford to dismiss it. He hurried to the crib and placed his hand on Elizabeth. Was she breathing? There was the slightest rising and falling in her little chest.

Or was there? He waited, measured, felt. Was she really breathing? Peter was unsure. He was about to call Kathleen when suddenly he seemed to hear a voice. Quiet as the rustling of the drapes. Beyond the darkness, there was a voice. Was it God? At a dairy farm in Pennsylvania? He felt Elizabeth's chest again. "Please breathe," he whispered to his child through his tears. Then, "Who are you?" he whispered to the presence he felt in the room.

With the drapes rustling and the room swaying, the silence and darkness were pierced by a voice that filled Peter's senses, and he heard the revealing words:

Do you love this child? Would you die to give her life? You have a sister, whom you shame and will not acknowledge. She is about to have a child whom you despise, yet she loves her unborn child just as you love this child. But I love both babies equally, for they are mine more than they are yours. You have despised this poor mother in your heart. You have called her a prostitute and made her crawl. You treasure your child but call hers illegitimate. There are no illegitimate children. You are a prideful man, giving value to things only as they have value to you. You would wish your child healthy? Her child needs your goodwill to live. Do you desire the tiny form beneath your hand to live? Repent of your callous indifference toward others whom I love. Call this woman you despise your sister. Acknowledge her unborn child to be one of your family. Then your own child will live.

Did Peter really hear this? Did these words come from the darkness of the room or only from the darkness of his heart? Had God come for a brief chat just prior to a plague of paralysis? He reached into the crib and touched the baby again. Was she breathing okay?

"Dear God," he said in a half whisper, "I beg you to let my child live."

Silence. Peter felt Elizabeth's arms and legs. Was there movement?

"Lord, I fully acknowledge my unnamed sister. Her child is *not* illegitimate. There are no illegitimate children. We are all one family, and you are the one true Father."

The baby beneath Peter's hand wriggled. She kicked his hand and began crying. Elizabeth was full of life, strong and moving around. Peter received his wonderful kicking child into his arms. He then laughed out loud, because for some unexplainable reason the light bulb came back on, with the same instant intensity his child had just sprung to life. Peter knew, however, his child now breathed and moved in response to his agreement to lay aside his indifference and unloving ways.

He laughed and waltzed all around the living room with Elizabeth in his arms. The child was laughing too. All the revelry woke up Kathleen in the other room.

"Peter, what's wrong?" cried Kathleen, rushing into the room.

"Wrong? Nothing's wrong!" Peter was smiling, and tears were streaming down his cheeks. He tossed Elizabeth up in the air. They both laughed.

"Peter, be careful! Remember, she's sick!"

"No, Kathleen. Our baby wasn't sick. I was."

"What are you saying?"

But he would tell her the story later. He instead handed Elizabeth to his wife, kissed them both, and turned and left the room.

Kathleen held her baby close and sat down to rock her back to sleep. She was surprised at how healthy and alert the child seemed. Kathleen was overjoyed to see the dramatic change. She bent low, her lips brushing her baby's tiny face, and spoke to her in baby talk.

Peter was talking too, though not in baby talk. He had some catching up to do with God. Was there a presence in the room? Had he heard voices? Oddly Peter remembered that Joan of Arc was burned at the stake for claiming something very similar.

He suspected it was the kind of mystery he would spend the rest of his life unraveling.

11

The following Monday, Ernest
approached Christine in the bottling room and
said, "I saw you in church yesterday sitting with
your mother."

"And I saw you, but without Helena."

"She wanted to come, but I told her she
needed to stay at home and rest, that she
shouldn't think she had to show up in church
just for God to take note of her attendance. But
I gotta ask you a question, Miss Christine,
about the pastor's sermon yesterday. Do you
think those men who threw Daniel into that
den of lions thought they were good Christians?"

"I imagine they thought they were good,
yes."

"How could they think that?"

"It's like the pastor said. It's usually the
good people who throw the best people to the

lions. Remember how he said the human race has an amazing ability to congratulate itself right into heaven. How faulty that thinking is! Have you ever met anyone who was trying to be a bad person, or even thought of himself as bad?"

"No, I guess I haven't."

"Me neither. What surprises me is that good Christians can read about the bad people of the Bible and never see any connection between themselves and the bad people who lived a long time ago, who also thought of themselves as good. I believe the people who never stop to see the similarity between themselves and the bad people of the Bible are actually a lot like those bad people. They just can't see it. Take my reputation, for example."

Ernest nodded.

"I'm sure most see me to be like that scarlet woman who Jesus met at the well, the woman with all the different husbands in her past, and the one she'd taken up with when Jesus met her wasn't even her husband. Well, I bet the good Christians at the church think of me as that woman but don't think of themselves as the self-righteous Pharisees who wanted to stone her."

"Shame on them," said Ernest.

"Maybe that's why many churches are so

ineffective. It seems lots of folks who go to church regularly think of themselves as good and so they don't see the similarities between themselves and all the bad people out there."

"Yes, ma'am," said Ernest.

"Now tell me, am I like the bad people of the Bible or more like the Lutherans around here?"

"You're more like the Lutherans, Miss Christine."

"Thank you, but they don't see me that way. Know what I believe?"

Ernest shrugged his shoulders.

"I believe that only the people who can say they're bad have any hope really of ever being good."

Ernest nodded and said, "I think I see what you mean."

He was about to say more when Isabel stuck her head through the doorway of the bottling room and said, "I'm off to town now. Is everything under control? I'll see you around. Be good."

"Funny, Miss Isabel, but we were just talking about that!" said Ernest.

"About being under control?"

"No, about being good. Miss Christine has a theory that only those people who can say they're bad are good. Does that make sense to you?"

"Mmm . . . not really."

"Explain it to her, Christine."

But Isabel didn't have time to hear the explanation.

After Isabel left, Christine continued to wash the milk bottles set out in front of her. As she scrubbed the insides with a brush, she glanced up at Ernest and said, "I've thought a lot about becoming a Christian, but I don't think I could ever think of myself as good enough. I've lived a bad life, Ernest."

"Sure, but you just said that the people who can say they're bad are the only ones that have a hope of being good. So if now you think of yourself as bad, maybe you're on the right road after all."

"Ernest, I'm an adulterer."

"Yes, ma'am. That's what they're saying around town."

Ernest didn't say what Christine wanted him to say. She was hoping he would protest the word. "But you know what's good about being seen as an adulterer?"

Ernest shrugged. "I guess I don't."

"Once people think the worst of you, there's nothing they have to guess about. There's a kind of freedom in it." Christine then paused a moment. She stopped her washing and stared at the ground and said almost to herself, "Still, sometimes I sit in church and I wonder when was the last time God showed up there."

Ernest nodded, said good-bye, and walked away.

Christine called after him, "Good-bye, Ernest. Thanks for listening to my rambling. Don't forget the pastor's sermon. It's the good people who pitch the best people to the lions."

But Ernest was gone before Christine finished.

It wasn't long before Christine had another visitor to the bottling room—Peter.

"How are you feeling?" he asked. When Christine said that she was feeling fine, he smiled. After asking twice about her health, he added, "Christine, I never want you to reveal our secret."

"Mr. McCaslin, we've been over all that. I promised and I keep my promises."

"I believe you. I must confess, I've not been all that kind to you. The truth is, I've been pretty bad. You heard the pastor's sermon yesterday?"

"I did. I was just talking about it with Ernest. I needed to hear what the pastor said. I've thought of nothing else since. I'm a bad woman, Mr. McCaslin."

"I'm not all that great myself. Maybe that's

when good becomes most possible—when someone like me can own up to being bad. I've thought a lot about those people who threw Daniel to the lions. Christine, I need to tell you that I'm the worst of men; the things in my heart are dark and evil. And one of the things that hurts me the most is the despicable way I treated you the day you came to my house with those photographs."

"Forgive me, Peter. I was the one in the wrong."

"I'm glad you're going to church."

"I'm not sure all the other Christians are."

"Ah, but they need you."

Christine smiled. "Because they can use me as an occasion to feel good about themselves."

Peter laughed. So did Christine. She sat there amazed at the fact that she and Peter were talking and laughing together. "Peter..." she started, "before when I tried to blackmail you, I—"

"Christine, I understand. Times are hard. You were desperate, and I was cruel. But it wasn't my cruelty that most concerned me—it was my pride and arrogance. Please forgive me. You are my sister; we had the same father."

"But, Mr. McCaslin—"

"Call me Peter. Brother, if you'd like."

"There's no need of that. What's happened

between our parents need never be a subject for the gossips. No, it may be true we're brother and sister, but as far as I'm concerned, Mama's dementia has forever taken that knowledge from the world. We're the only ones who know, and the secret is better left with God."

"Maybe you're right. The truth getting out might hurt the memories of our parents. That aside, I promise you all my support and love. You're my sister and my equal, and you'll always be welcome in my home. As long as I'm around, you and your baby will never want for anything." Peter stopped and turned to leave. Then he turned back and said, "Isabel tells me the roof on your house needs repair. I'll send one of the hands around to look it over and see what kind of repairs it needs."

"You'd do that? I haven't any money."

"We'll find a way to fix it. The main thing is, I don't want you to think you're out there all by yourself trying to make ends meet. Especially with Mabel to look after and the baby on the way. From now on, no more struggling by yourself."

Christine smiled. "Mr. McCaslin ... Peter, thank you. I want you to know I'm going to be a good worker here at the dairy. I'm going to church too, and when my baby is born, I want the baby to be baptized."

"The child's going to need a godfather, then. I'd be happy to submit my name as a possible candidate."

Christine smiled again. "There's no need to look any further—you've got the job! It looks like I've not only gained a brother, I've also gained a friend. Again, thank you."

"Thank you. For forgiving me, and for allowing me the privilege of being a part of your life, and soon the privilege of helping you to raise your son or daughter. So, thinking of the past and everything we've been through, I'd like to propose that we start over, this time as brother and sister. What do you say?"

Overcome by Peter's words, Christine nodded and then reached to take his hand.

Instead, Peter embraced her.

Midmorning on Friday Ingrid
went to the mailbox. Inside was a letter from
Stroope, Stroope and Geraint. She guessed it
contained the reply to the manuscript Otto
recently sent to the publisher. She hoped it
wouldn't be just another rejection; there had
been too many already. She didn't want to pry
into his affairs, yet she could think of no other
way to know for sure what the letter said. So
she decided to open it. It opened quite easily.
Pulling the letter from its envelope with no
trouble at all, she started reading.

Dear Mr. Mueller:

*With a great deal of anticipation, we have
agreed in our recent publication board meeting
that your poetry must have a place in our catalogue of books. We will be sending you a contract
that offers you an advance of a thousand dollars*

upon signing and a second thousand dollars upon publication. Your book will be listed in our spring catalogue, advertising its release in early summer. Other conditions of our agreement will appear in the contract that will be arriving by post within a few days.

We are most anxious that you sign and return the contract to us at your earliest convenience so that we may proceed with all expedition toward its publication.

Congratulations, Mr. Mueller. It will be wonderful to have your poetry as a part of the fine books of Stroope, Stroope and Geraint.

Sincerely,
Ralph Royce, Editor

Ingrid felt no guilt for having snooped. It's not so bad snooping if what you find by doing so is joyous news. She hid Otto's letter in the bread box and waited for him to come home. She was glad it was Friday, because Erick would be coming home too. It would do Erick much good to celebrate his brother's good fortune.

Erick was still not himself. Though it seemed to Ingrid that he was gradually coming to terms with losing Mary, the intervening weeks had been miserable times of reflection for Erick, and with Ingrid's own dark moods of grief, the Muellers had certainly seen happier days. This would surely be such a day.

She decided to fix knackwurst and kraut. It was always Hans's favorite—after wiener schnitzel and cabbage—and now that he was gone, it somehow brought the whole family closer by enjoying what Hans used to enjoy. Marguerite was the real objector; she didn't like the sausage and sauerkraut one bit. When Hans was alive, she would share her negative opinion of his favorite German food right to his face, causing Hans to roll with laughter.

Marguerite was the first in after school. On coming through the door and smelling the boiling kraut, she frowned and said, "Grandma, instead can I have an apple-butter sandwich tonight?"

"Well, yes, but you'll have to eat it while the rest of us have wurst and kraut."

"Okay. Know who's got the polio, Grandma?"

Marguerite had an odd way of phrasing things, but Ingrid came to attention because of the seriousness of the epidemic disease. "No. Who, Marguerite?"

"Zelpha Denman, that's who. My teacher said it all started when Zelpha got a cold and couldn't stand up. She said if ever we catch a cold, we should stay home and not try to come to school."

"That's right, Marguerite. And you must not

play with anybody who has a cold. Now go read your fairy-tale book while I finish fixing supper. Tonight we've got something special to celebrate!"

With Marguerite engrossed in her book, Ingrid went to work in getting everything ready for the big night. Soon it was nearing five-thirty. She must hurry and set the table. She decided to use the good china, including candles. Just as she finished arranging everything, the doorbell rang.

Ingrid rushed to the door, the whole way racking her brain who it could be this late in the day. She almost wished she didn't have to answer it, but of course she did. She swung the door open.

"Mary!" The last person in the world Ingrid expected to see this night was Mary Withers, yet she was one of the people she most wanted to see. "And Alexis too! It's so good to see you! Do come in."

"Alexis?" cried Marguerite as she flew into the living room from the back of the house. "Oh, Alexis, I missed you!"

"Hi, Marguerite! I missed you too."

"I'm so glad you're here."

"We're moving back and we're never leaving again!" Alexis announced.

"Is this true, Mary?" asked Ingrid. "Are you moving back to town?"

Mary nodded and bit her lip. "Ingrid . . . I'm afraid I've made a big mistake. I met Alicia Withers this week and . . . well, I've been such a fool. I guess at first when I saw Ted, I saw Tom. Believe me, as it turns out, they were nothing alike. Ted is morally flawed. Yet without thinking I let myself and Alexis—" Then Mary broke into tears and fell into Ingrid's arms. Neither of the women said anything for a matter of minutes as Mary gradually regained her composure. "Ingrid, tell me you forgive me."

"Mary, we all make mistakes. You don't even need to ask if we forgive you. You were taken in, that's all. But let's not speak of it further. Now you're home and your presence in this town is a gift."

Mary gave Ingrid a look of gratitude.

"Mary," said Ingrid, "do you think you still have feelings for Erick?" Ingrid realized she was being forward, but she also realized that at any moment her son would be walking through the front door, and if Mary wasn't open to the restoration of their love, she must leave before Erick got home. As much as Ingrid loved Mary, she could not bear to see her son's old wounds get reopened by his seeing Mary once again.

"I don't think I've ever quit loving your son.

Only gradually did I come to see that I could never be content with anybody but Erick Mueller. I knew that in time I would have to work up the courage to get away from Ted and come home, but for so long I was afraid of his anger. Then Alicia Withers called, and she told me everything. How you came to the truth through the personals in the paper. Ingrid, thank you for coming to my rescue."

Ingrid reached out and patted her hand.

Mary continued. "It seemed impossible that Alicia could actually be his wife. But when I realized she was a woman deeply suffering from all that she had to carry, I came to a moment of honesty. I knew I had to risk Ted's anger. When he came in that night, Alicia and I both greeted him. The blood drained from his face. Then just as quickly as he paled, he reddened again. He clenched his fists and stepped toward Alicia as though he might actually strike her.

" 'Don't, Ted!' I told him. I was surprised to hear myself speak with such firmness. I said to him, 'I talked to the sheriff, and he assured me that if you hurt any of us, he'll lock you up.'

"Then he turned on me and said, 'Get out, Mary! Go back to your stupid little town and poverty.' So I ran and got my bags, which were already packed, grabbed Alexis by the hand, and left. As sorry as I feel for Alicia, I'm so relieved to be free of that horrible man. Oh, Ingrid, how could I have been so blind? So completely taken in? And I've hurt Erick terribly. He must despise me."

"Quite to the contrary, Mary. Erick has never stopped loving you. He's been miserable since you two broke up. Trust me, my boy is desperately in love with you and he—"

Ingrid heard footsteps on the porch. "Quick, Mary, it must be Otto! Let's surprise him."

But it was not Otto. Suddenly Erick walked in.

"Mary!" he said, a stunned expression on his face. "Mary!" he said again, and his eyes filled with tears.

"Erick...!" Her voice choked and her tears ran freely before she could squeeze out anything else.

When she began to cry, Erick took her in his arms and they both wept, even though Erick didn't understand everything yet.

"Erick, we've come home for good," said Mary.

"Just like that? Every day I've asked God for such a miracle. It never came. Then now, all at once, like this. Mary, I love you!"

"I love you. But I'm so embarrassed by my foolish infatuation and all that took place with

Ted. I don't see how you could ever forgive me, let alone still love me."

"Loving you isn't something I could ever stop and start. It's been in place, waiting and hoping." They kissed, not caring that Ingrid was watching. When their kiss had extended overlong, Ingrid cleared her throat, calling them back to the world at hand. Mary and Erick laughed, then walked to the couch and sat down. "Welcome home, my darling Mary," said Erick. "I must not ever lose this dream again."

Ingrid could hardly believe her good fortune. She thought of Hans. *Look down from heaven, you wonderful old German, and see this miracle God has given us. Oh, Hans! Our boys are alive again. I don't wish you back; I only want you to look down and see the Mueller world made whole again.* Her reverie was interrupted by Alexis and Marguerite running back into the living room.

"Grandma, can Alexis and Mary eat dinner with us?"

"Mary. . . ?" pleaded Ingrid. "We have plenty."

Mary nodded.

"Yes," agreed Erick. "Stay and have dinner with us!"

"Goodie!" cried Marguerite.

There was one thing more Ingrid had to do.

She went straight to the phone and called Isabel and invited her to dinner too. She asked her to hurry right over and told her there would be a wonderful surprise for everyone.

After hanging up, Ingrid told Erick and Mary to make themselves comfortable and get all caught up on their lives. She walked to the kitchen to add three more place settings to the table. *Otto, where are you?* she thought. But she was content to wait. She quickly prepared a pie-crust under her roller, took out some apples she had just canned, added the necessary ingredients, sprinkled on cinnamon, and then stuck the pie in the oven.

Never had she felt richer. She could hear the little girls laughing in Marguerite's bedroom. Mary and Erick were sitting quietly on the couch, their heads close together. This would be the perfect meal! The potatoes were bubbling in the pan, the knackwurst was steaming, the candles were burning. But the coffee—she must make the coffee! There's no perfect dinner without fresh coffee. So she reached for the coffee beans and the grinder and turned on one of the stove's burners. After she had the coffee going, she peeked at the pie. It smelled heavenly.

Ingrid felt strange in doing it, but it was the week of Thanksgiving and she was too full of joy not to have a moment with Hans. So she took a walk to the cemetery, and when she finally approached his modest headstone, she laid a half dozen asters before it and whispered, "Here, Hans. These are for you. I barely saved them from last night's frost."

She knew he wouldn't much care for the flowers, but she brought them for him anyway. "It's cold this morning. You'd like it—there'll be a lot of people burning coal. You'd be proud of us, my darling. We're selling coal and lots of it, and we're not giving any of it away. Well, maybe a little. To the Cartwrights, that's all. Oh, and I also sent a half ton to the Stones. You don't mind, do you? Things are hard for them since Mr. Stone lost his leg to diabetes."

Ingrid paused a moment.

"Otto is finally going to get published, received his first payment of a thousand dollars. And you said he'd better quit writing poetry and keep delivering coal." Ingrid knew Hans was in heaven, yet that was no reason for her not to remind him that he'd been wrong about Otto's writing. "Hans, this is the best news of all. Otto and Erick are both going to be married on the same day, the second Sunday of Advent. Erick will be moving into Mary's old place, and Otto and Isabel are going to build their own house in the spring. When Otto gets the money for his book, he'll have a pretty good start on buying the materials. Peter McCaslin is going to help."

Ingrid could almost hear Hans say in a surprised voice, *What! Peter McCaslin?*

"Yes, Hans. Peter McCaslin! He's changed! Just in time too, because it looks like the cow people and the coal people are going to be part of the same family come Christmas. I don't know what's come over the man, but he's different and in a good way. Isabel says he's been reformed like Ebenezer Scrooge. He even volunteered to have the wedding reception out at the big house. It should be lovely. He told Isabel he'd pay for the whole thing.

"Hans, I'm going to hand over the coal business to Otto and Erick. Is that okay? I'm thinking Otto could run it most of the time, and Erick could maybe use his summers when he's not teaching to get the business ready for the fall."

Ingrid looked down at the asters lying on the frost-covered grave. How she wished Hans could be with her for all of the wonderful things that were about to unfold for their family. "Dearest Hans," she said, staring at the headstone, "I have missed you more than you can imagine. How I loved you. . . ."

She turned to leave the cemetery. She never said good-bye to Hans. She never would. She needed him as she always had, and there was no use saying good-bye when she felt she would soon be greeting him in person. For the moment Ingrid had important things to do. She had a most pressing matter to discuss with Isabel.

Arriving at the coal office, Ingrid was glad to see Isabel was there talking with Christine about the upcoming wedding. But the delicate matter Ingrid had to settle with Isabel was a matter she had to keep hidden from Christine.

"Isabel," said Ingrid, "would you take a walk with me? I need your good opinion on something."

Isabel said yes, and the two of them left the coal office.

When they were comfortably out of earshot of Christine, Ingrid reached in her coat pocket and pulled out an envelope and handed it to Isabel. "There's forty dollars in there. I've somehow managed to save the money, and I want you to use it to replace what you borrowed from Christine's baby fund without her knowing it."

"Oh, Ingrid, but it's not your debt. It was I who took the money. I'll figure out a way to pay it back. By the way, Benny sent me another forty for Christine just this past week. He truly must have changed his ways. And my brother also has promised to help her, so she will surely have all the support she needs. You know he's even repaired her roof? I declare, Ingrid, I don't know what's happening. The whole world seems to be improving right before our eyes." Isabel held out the envelope to Ingrid and said, "But I'd rather you keep this money for yourself. I'll figure out something."

"Please, Isabel. Times are hard; accept the money. I'm soon to be your mother-in-law, and you wouldn't want to start your marriage with in-law problems, would you?" Ingrid smiled, then said, "I insist that you take the money!"

Isabel agreed, if only to keep the peace.

"Now, let's go sit down somewhere together and have tea. I have some suggestions to make concerning the wedding. They're good suggestions. You don't mind my making suggestions, do you?"

"No, of course not. But—"

"Because I don't want to be too pushy."

"Of course not."

"Good. I would never presume to interfere with your wedding plans, and yet there are a couple of things that—"

"That seem to be worthy presumptions." Isabel smiled.

"Oh, all right. I do want to presume, maybe even push a little."

"Push away," laughed Isabel.

"Let's go out for tea and I'll tell you ... I mean, I'll suggest what I have in mind. We'll have to hurry. I still have to call on Mary. She needs a little help with these things too, you know. Mary is more independent than you are, so I'll need to be a tiny bit more firm when I make suggestions for her."

"Ingrid, you should know that Mary and I have been doing some planning on our own. Nothing major. We've just been talking about what we're going to wear and—"

"That sounds major to me. I hope you haven't decided on anything I can't live with."

"Me too. If we have, you'll just have to help us undecide."

"Oh, I would never presume to interfere, Isabel."

Isabel cocked her eyebrow and chuckled. "Of course not."

"Of course not," repeated Ingrid with a grin.

While approaching the restaurant where they planned to have their tea, they saw Mary walking down the street.

"Mary! What luck!" Ingrid called. "Do you have time for tea? We need to talk!"

Mary did, and Ingrid felt elated about how the day was turning out. She decided she would work at not being too forward. She must drop in a suggestion or two and then somehow make them think it was their idea. Yes, that's what she would do.

Then, as the three women stepped inside the restaurant, Ingrid was surprised to hear herself say, "Mary, I've a nice wicker cornucopia we could place on the gift table at the reception."

14

Some, including Ingrid, said that
Helena Pitovsky, now feeling much recovered
from her illness, looked a bit out of place pour-
ing the punch. Ingrid had loaned Helena one
of her better dresses, yet still the poor woman
appeared out of her element—socially speaking.
Helena's shyness made her prefer to watch
from the back where the crowd wouldn't notice
her. But Isabel stepped in and insisted that she
serve the main beverage to all the guests,
despite Ingrid's feeling a little uncomfortable
with the arrangement. So Helena served.

Where Isabel and Ingrid really differed was
whether Christine Cartwright ought to keep
the guest book and gift registry. Given Christine's reputation, Ingrid felt that having Christine in charge of these things might be deemed
as inappropriate by certain of their guests and
so could be off-putting. There was also the

matter of the illegitimate baby that she carried. Again Isabel stood firm, reminding Ingrid that there were no illegitimate babies and that Christine needed to be included. Ingrid apologized and gave in.

Isabel had bought Christine a new navy blue dress to wear, which looked real nice with the imitation pearls Christine had picked out. Her makeup was applied with too heavy a hand—which reminded Ingrid of how she used to make her living—but Ernest, who was glad to see her keeping the guest book, told her, "You look mighty pretty today, Miss Christine."

"Do you think so?" Christine said, pumping the conversation to get the most she could out of Ernest's compliment. Not counting the kind things Isabel had said, it was the only compliment she'd gotten, and she was quite grateful for it.

Alexis and Marguerite carried the rings and strewed the rose petals. Erick and Mary said their *I do*'s just before Isabel and Otto did. Mrs. Schmidt played the organ proudly, and Ursula Hess sang "O Promise Me" and "The Lord's Prayer." And then Pastor Stoltzfus preached a fine wedding sermon.

The reception at the McCaslin place couldn't have turned out more beautiful. The Frankmann Trio played the cello, oboe, and piano. Both of the Mueller boys danced with their new brides, and then other couples joined in, including Peter and Kathleen and then Peter and Isabel. Every breath stopped when Peter walked to Christine and took her hand. Christine was bewildered but smiled as Peter led her to the center of the room. It was one of those new two-step dances, and Christine danced as though she practiced every day.

The two couples drove to Philadelphia in Peter's new DeSoto sedan, which he was generous enough to lend to the boys. It was as close as they could come to a limousine. He assured the newlyweds that they could keep the car for as long as they wanted to extend their honeymoons. But a single night of splurging was about all they could afford. The couples spent the night in the same hotel in Philadelphia. In some ways it seemed to Isabel and Mary more like a double date than a honeymoon.

The following morning was Sunday, and Ingrid was eager to show up at church and rehearse the glory of the previous day with all her friends. When she rose to get dressed she was amazed to find it snowing. The second snow of the season, and it was ample. In fact, it had been snowing all night. The snow piled up so thick that Ingrid decided she would have to wait until the next Lord's Day to have everyone celebrate the wedding with her.

Marguerite was still asleep in her room. Ingrid knew, however, that the moment Marguerite awoke, the day's solitude would be swallowed whole.

But for the moment it was silent, so she tiptoed to the kitchen and made herself a cup of tea. She was nearly through with it when it occurred to her that it was the second week of Advent. She read from her prayer book and enjoyed the pre-Christmas passage very much. After a second cup of tea, she stood and walked to the window.

She stared at the falling snow and said softly, "Oh, Hans, I miss you." She knew out at the cemetery, Hans's headstone would be drifted about by white. Hans liked the snow, for it meant the townspeople would buy his coal.

She liked snow too. The snow made a chiffon dessert out of frozen raindrops. It got the world ready for a formal party. Snow eased boundaries and connected the slums with the manor houses. It brought the realms of coal people and cow people together and gave bright, clean hope a chance to lie on the ground and sparkle.

Ingrid had sons.

Ingrid had daughters.

Ingrid had grandchildren.

Ingrid had a husband whose memory forged her eagerness for heaven. "It's snowing. Are you happy, Hans?" She knew he was. "I hope to see you ... but it might be a while. In the meantime I think I'll bake a strudel."

Soon the house was full of the aroma of spices, and King of Prussia seemed a great place to transform mere apples into strudel. The nature of all things had been altered, so why not apples?

Her mood was high. The spices made her heady.

Was there trouble anywhere?

There are days when cinnamon strudel can change the world. It wasn't just the apples that were transformed. The spices floated out across the snow, and the very odor made King of Prussia appear new to the senses.

After all, a stick of cinnamon's a mighty thing!

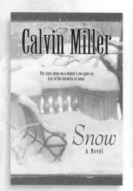